HARD OPTION

Gwen Moffat

CHIVERS LARGE PRINT
BATH

British Library Cataloguing in Publication Data available

This Large Print edition published by Chivers Press, Bath, 2003.
Published by arrangement with the author.

U.K. Hardcover ISBN 0 7540 7224 X
U.K. Softcover   ISBN 0 7540 7225 8

Printed and bound in Great Britain by
Antony Rowe Ltd., Chippenham, Wiltshire

HARD OPTION

CHAPTER ONE

The search was resumed at first light on Sunday. The gale was moderating now and the cloud ceiling lay at two thousand feet. The missing pair were a man and his schoolboy son who had set out for a mountain walk on Friday in deteriorating weather. They didn't return to their hotel for dinner, but guests who lost themselves and came down late were a common occurrence, and the hotelier waited for a while before he informed the police. He did so at ten-thirty and by then it was too late for the rescuers to go out that night.

A full-scale search on Saturday covered the range the walkers had intended to traverse but found no trace of them. The gale increased and through Saturday night a number of young soldiers were in trouble in an adjacent area and two rescue teams were diverted to bring down the Army casualties who were suffering from exposure. Dawn on Sunday found only Owen Parry's team from Minera left to look for the two civilians: a team no longer at its best after only a few hours' rest. Moreover, they were subdued and resentful because, since their quarry wasn't on one range, the one which had been their stated intention, they could be anywhere. The search had no focal point.

'Perhaps they went home,' Keith Williams suggested, recalling a couple who had decided to do just that and never turned up at the youth hostel where they'd booked places. Three teams had searched for two days until word came that the missing pair had merely changed their plans.

'For God's sake!' Parry exclaimed, the fatigue showing through, but only with Keith. 'You're still asleep. They've left all their gear at the hotel, and the wife's on her way here. It's a straightforward job this time: they're dead or holed up somewhere, in an old sheep pen perhaps, sheltering.'

'Two dead? And it's a long time to spend in shelter: the pair of them, without one going for help—two nights and a day.' Parry looked at the other thoughtfully. 'They must be separated,' Keith went on, 'and we missed them. Both of them.' He grinned slyly.

Parry looked past him bleakly and raised his voice. 'Teams specialise—you ought to know that by now. Searching isn't our scene, not in the ordinary way, and when we have to do it we're caught with our pants down. We're not much cop on cliff rescues either—' he waited for his hearers to assume expressions of acute boredom and went on, '—but we're a bit better on rock than on a sweep search.' He suppressed a sigh, thinking that sweeps were usually ineffective because the searchers thought they were looking for a body, so they

2

were casual and missed a chap who might still be alive. It was not surprising that when a body was found, it was almost invariably on ground that had been covered more than once already. His own men hated sweep searches: too meticulous, too demanding on discipline—and subject to failure. How could you sweep boulder fields and broken hillsides in cloud when people suffering from exposure crawled into the backs of holes and hid themselves away to die? Parry didn't like searching either; there was no danger. What he liked, and the men adored, were the big cliff rescues. Normally sweep searches on easy but dull ground were left to the lesser teams and volunteers who couldn't be trusted on rock.

*   *   *

He took them up the hill slowly that Sunday morning. Speed, after a breakfast at five o'clock, would have had them retching with nausea. A slow guide's pace worked the stiffness out of them gradually, giving them time to adjust to a new day which was nothing more than a lessening of the dark. Despite their subdued and unusual silence, he was confident that they retained enough of their reserves to give him a working margin in an emergency.

The valley was almost enclosed by a horseshoe of peaks which culminated, at the

3

back of the skyline, in Carnedd Iago, a mountain of three thousand feet. Under one horn of this cirque was a cliff, a big cliff. It could be the wrong place to look because people walking round the Skyline Route normally started on the ridge above the cliff, and most people came to grief at the end of their walk. But these were all suppositions, attempts to find fixed points from which to work; in mountains it was always the unpredictable that happened and the team had to be taken *somewhere* even if it was anywhere. A cliff could contain diversions; moors and boulder fields held nothing more than boredom.

All day yesterday it had rained and most of the men possessed only one set of clothing so that now, sweating inside their waterproofs, they were hot and uncomfortable in clothes that were damp when they started. All carried heavy loads.

They moved up the side of the cliff and the cloud closed in on them. After a while Parry realised that the rain had stopped. The wet rock gleamed in a translucent ivory light and their world was composed of shades of slate through which they moved as a file of muted colour: rose and lemon waterproofs, and helmets like bulbous flowers. He kept glancing back and down at them automatically as one always did with parties, however competent, and he noted with satisfaction that they were

4

going a little better now that they were getting into their stride. He reckoned he could call on a further eight hours' work from them before they had to be rested again.

Above him he could hear the wind on the summit ridge, a dry wind without the sweep of rain. With luck it would clear soon.

On the ridge the rocks were clean and polished by the nails of the old-timers' boots which had whitened the rock like a blazed trail. They turned to the last steep rise, going neatly now: stepping up, not plodding. The atmosphere was better on top; on the ascent he'd felt starved for air.

He wondered how long he should stay here waiting for the mist to clear. If it did shift, he could have made a mistake in coming to Craig y Castell for, given good visibility, they'd be in the wrong place to study the cliff face. A number of ledges, if not most of them, would be hidden from view, not to mention all the cracks and chimneys where a falling body might lodge, the caves in the backs of gullies where an injured man might have crawled for shelter. But—two of them? One always assumed that they'd be found together: a missing pair; in practice they were often separated and sometimes by long distances: the one collapsed, the other gone on for help, but usually in the wrong direction.

He saw a foot first. Not that he recognised it as a foot: an oddly-shaped rock, too dark for rock, then the outline of a sole, and as he distinguished the pattern of rubber cleats and knew it for a boot, he saw that the shape behind was fawn, not grey: a body among the rocks. The man lay a few yards below the cairn, asleep or dead. He was alone.

Parry glanced round automatically but didn't tell the others to look further for the boy, not yet. If he'd been anywhere in the vicinity, he'd have been by his father. Gareth Lloyd, the First Aider, came up and knelt by the man's head.

'Alive?' Parry asked, without hope.

Gareth shrugged. The victim wore no gloves. He was feeling for the pulse, touching the forehead.

'He's warm.'

'Christ!' someone exclaimed, and giggled. 'After two nights out!'

Parry turned. 'Haven't you got the bag out yet?' he asked viciously, and the group shifted, swinging rucksacks to the ground, starting to unpack. The leader knelt on the other side of the casualty and took stock of the grey face scored by deep lines. It was a fine-boned face with sunken eye sockets and an aquiline nose. The eyelids lifted with infinite effort, lowered, lifted again.

'Rescue?' The sound was like an exhaled breath.

'You're all right now,' Gareth assured him.

'Charles?'

'Your boy?'

'He's all right? He got down safely?'

Gareth looked at his leader.

'Which way did he go?' Parry asked.

The eyes turned and stared at him and Parry watched the incised lines in the cheeks soften as the spirit faded. In the silence a gust of wind smashed against a wall below.

'Not very strong.' Gareth's tone was loaded, warning. He, too, looked at the leader. He was referring to the man's pulse.

'Which way did Charles go?' The First Aider probed reluctantly because there was no way you could do it without making the man suffer now that he knew his boy hadn't got down.

'Down the gully; I wondered at the time . . .'

'Down the gully,' a voice murmured. 'He just walked down the bloody gully.'

Parry stood up, stretching his legs, and stared at the speaker. The others watched him and waited. Behind him Gareth supervised the transferring of the victim to the opened casualty bag. The radio operator was moving about the cairn trying to call Base for the stretcher. Leaving the others to zip the bag, Gareth stood up and, taking Parry's elbow, turned him away from the group and spoke quietly.

'I think he just died.'

'Resuscitation?'

'After two nights out? It was only the

7

thought of his lad kept him alive. We'll try it though if it'll make you happier.'

Parry glanced at the other sharply. 'You try. We'll look for the boy.'

The cloud was thinning spasmodically. This summit was a miniature peak on its own with two or three shallow gullies running up to a terminal rock platform. They'd scrambled up one of the gullies to the casualty, and another, initially as innocuous when viewed from the top, dropped away on the east. After fifty feet it debouched on a sloping ledge and below that was the cliff. It wouldn't be the first time that someone had mistaken the eastern gully for the walkers' way down. Usually they fell to the bottom.

Through holes in the mist they could see the foot of the screes a thousand feet below but not the slopes immediately underneath them. They strung out along the summit ridge, looking for vantage points from which they might glimpse at least some of the more obvious ledges, but all they could see down there were rocks and clumps of tired vegetation. It was the end of summer and the flowers were over.

Parry stopped trying to see what lay below and looked from one to the other of his team as they approached and retreated from the edge or lowered themselves over the lip for a better view of something that attracted their attention. The mist came back and mocked them but before it obscured one stationary figure, Parry felt the cool stir of excitement in his belly like the start of a long and sustained and beautiful orgasm, and he moved down the rocks to Keith Williams who was ignoring the rabble peering over the edge and waiting for the leader because he'd been promised this moment for weeks past.

He was stroking his helmet absently and turned at Parry's approach. 'Ready?' he asked impertinently, as if he were the leader instead of the newest recruit to the team. 'We're wasting time; we've got to get on the cliff.'

'You're too eager,' Parry said, knowing he couldn't crush the other, not wanting to.

'But I need the experience.' The lad's eyes were dancing as he buckled his helmet.

'You'll come to a bad end,' Parry said. 'You're too cocky by half. Get a radio and a rope while I see Gareth—and test the radio first.'

*   *   *

The two of them climbed unroped down an arête which wasn't technically hard, but, with a smear of slime on the rock and every runnel streaming water, they had to concentrate to the full on their points of contact. A slip when only one hand was on a poor and greasy hold could prove fatal—but then that could be the case at any time. The difference here was that they weren't fresh, the rock was wet, and they were unroped. For the most part they didn't rope on rescues; there was never time to observe the rules. Below their boots the cliff heeled over into space.

They must have been some two hundred feet from the top when Keith said: 'There's something in the gully.'

Parry eased his way out of a chimney and looked sideways. 'Where?'

'Above that cave. It's square, yellow—see? What the hell is it?'

He saw it then: a gaudy yellow rectangle poised on a stone. It appeared to move slightly in the breeze.

'It looks like a sponge, a bit of sponge rubber. It could be a pad from a rucksack strap.'

'It looks new.'

'It hasn't been there long. Keep going, we can get into the gully from the Terrace.'

They descended another hundred feet to a big ledge and traversed across a wall into the gully which wasn't vertical at this point. It was full of vegetation and the plants had been newly crushed into the bed. In one place bared soil was smoothed and curved from the impact of a heavy weight.

'He passed this way,' Keith said facetiously. He was quieter now, feeling the loneliness, dreading the wreck of a human being that they must soon find, if it wasn't on the screes.

Below them the strip of vegetation was a green chute terminating at a lip of rock. The rock was rain-washed and held no marks of blood or shreds of skin.

'Find a belay,' Parry murmured, 'and give me a top rope.'

The rock was shattered here, and there were no solid spikes to put the rope round. He watched Keith testing rickety flakes and knew that if he came off himself, he'd take the other with him . . . and all this was consuming valuable time—if the missing boy were still alive. Parry considered. The boy had fallen three hundred feet when he reached this point. Not fallen, he corrected himself, bounced. He could still be above the bottom if he'd lodged somewhere; he might be just below them, unconscious.

'Leave it,' he ordered. 'We'll go down from the Terrace and traverse in again.'

'What! Go down Lacewing?'

'You first. You can descend a Severe on a rope.'

'He'll be at the bottom!'

Parry ignored him and started to lead the way back to the Terrace. He didn't mind the lad being frightened of a body but he'd have to become accustomed to working on steep rock. The fear had some foundation in fact; it was one thing to descend a route that was nothing more than a scramble, even in the wet, but a different concept to be ordered to climb down

11

the hard way. You had to be ruthless with them: make them face their own terror. Keith would adjust—in time.

There was a good peg driven into a crack on the Terrace. Parry had put it there three years ago when they'd been forced to lower an Army officer with a fractured femur. He clipped into the peg and sent Keith down the top pitch of Lacewing.

A pretty name, he thought idly as the rope ran out: a pretty climb. He remembered the delicate holds on the wall which would have to be reversed when his turn came—and without a top rope. He yawned and looked at Carn Goch diagonally across the other side of the combe with mist playing about its summit screes but sun and cloud shadows drifting across the lower crags: nice, warm, dry crags with big holds. He could see the roof of Dolwen, his own cottage, among its sheltering sycamores, and something white in the garden. Beryl had done the washing; unusual, on a Sunday, but then she'd have put his wet clothes on the line to dry, and decided to make a job of it. His father would disapprove when he came up for lunch. Washing on Sunday! Parry grimaced and thought of his men on the summit. He wondered if Gareth had given up trying to resuscitate the casualty.

It was very quiet on the cliff. The wind had died away and the rest of the day should be pleasant . . . They weren't going to have

12

enough carriers. One stretcher for the chap on top, another for the boy—but if the boy was dead, they could leave him until tomorrow. They didn't need to make excuses; it would take the rest of the day to get the other one down from the summit. Parry looked at his watch. It was only eight-thirty! He'd forgotten how early they'd started. They'd have time to get both casualties down after all . . . It wouldn't do the team any good: two corpses. He wondered if there was anything he could do about that; he didn't want the morale of the men to drop.

Keith shouted that he was down. Parry waited until the lad had found a belay, then unclipped from the peg and, holding the rope so that it wasn't taut to him, moved to the edge. Eighty feet below, on a diminutive ledge, Keith appeared, foreshortened, staring upwards.

It was a bad finishing hold (which, in reverse, of course, became the initial one): friction for only one hand on a rounded lump, nothing for the other until you were on the wall and could reach down to waist level. The wall was just on vertical. Parry inhaled deeply and turned inwards with resigned composure to face the rock. He felt blindly for the first foothold, chided himself, recalled its position, felt again and found it. 'God!' he gasped softly, and lowered himself on the friction hold.

13

As his other hand came down and closed on the good solid flake at waist level, he relaxed—then checked himself. Lack of concentration now could mean a clear drop of five hundred feet: catapulting his second out from the cliff. There was no security on this pitch. No, Keith wouldn't go with him; his belay was good—but the rope would have to break under the shock-load.

He stopped and retracted his consciousness, focusing deliberately on the texture of the rock in front of his eyes. Something was wrong; he'd descended Severes before. Was it fatigue? He felt good and light, not torpid. The smell of death? He sniffed and thought he detected the stink of putrescence. In the gully or below there could be a corpse. His mind was shrinking from this. Then the mind must become subservient. It was his *body* going down this wall: toes, fingers, muscle, bone. Part of him knew and loved Lacewing; a fine machine was descending the top pitch under its own power. It knew what to do without the direction of his will so, if for a moment he doubted himself, the body could operate independently and with confidence. There was nothing to fear; a corpse was a shell.

He descended the smooth bit carefully and correctly, feeling his fingers damp on the holds but scorning to wipe the sweat off on his breeches. He looked down and was surprised to see that Keith should appear so much

14

nearer after only a few feet. Climbing was all psychological; on the wrong side of the hard move the drop was stupendous, ledges were too tiny even to arrest a fall, one's second was a novice and the rope a thread of gossamer. Far below, yet so near you could feel the impact—the screes waited like the maw of Death: magnetic, but now, with the hard move above and, underneath, a neat and adequate sequence of holds to step down lightly, the drop had become an exhilaration, the ledge on which his second stood was large and level—and Keith himself was a promising lad who would benefit from the experience.

His second was suffering though. Nearing the ledge, Parry's glance encountered the other's naked eyes, still fearful from watching that initial move when the lad would have known that a mistake, a slip, would have been the end for his leader and, not being knowledgeable about the breaking strain of ropes, would have thought that the fall would drag him off as well. Parry smiled gently at him and saw the wide eyes contract a little and the mouth, which had been stretched in a rictus, relax in the ghost of a response. The leader nodded to himself and tore his gaze away, his mind to the shared objective—and then he hardened because there was no conscious need to focus on the job: the focus was there, in the gully.

It was his second body in a very short time

but this one was far more shocking in its curious but curiously familiar attitude: twisted, at least in the lower limbs, spread-eagled, and still.

'I didn't see him,' Keith babbled. 'I was watching you all the time. I never took my eyes off you.'

'It's all right. It wouldn't have made any difference.'

They walked along the ledge and into the gully. As their boots ground on the stones they saw a hand, dark and lacerated, move limply.

'He's alive,' Keith whispered.

*　　　*　　　*

The diagnosis which, generally, he shrank from because it was so easy to make a mistake, was simple this time. The rain had washed the hair clean and the wounds showed through, and both legs were so crazily awry that the pelvis was probably shattered, but skull and pelvis seemed secondary considerations for the spine was out of alignment.

He used the radio to ask for the stretcher and the best climbers to be sent down, but not Gareth. He had a poor opinion of the First Aider's standard on rock; he'd be a liability descending the cliff.

The casualty had said nothing although for a few minutes after their arrival he had been conscious, his eyes following their movements.

16

It was doubtful if he could have spoken had he wanted to because the jaw was badly damaged. Parry thought that he had never seen a body so broken and still alive. Keith had been sick.

There was nothing they could do until the First Aid rucksack was brought down and even that seemed superfluous. Parry supposed that to splint the legs would ensure easier transference to the stretcher but how did you transfer this one without causing further damage to the spine? They should put a helmet on him for protection against falling stones too. He stared at the battered head in disgust.

Keith, pale and sweating, tried to redeem himself: 'You don't need to put a hat on him, not with the shield.'

Parry glanced at him, nodded approval, and went back on the air to tell Gareth to be sure to send down the plastic shield, to have it brought from Base immediately if it hadn't come up with the stretcher.

'How long do you reckon they'll be?' Keith asked. His distaste for staying in that place was obvious. He was suffering from shock. They moved away from the gully and spoke in low voices.

'We'll go back to the Terrace and start preparing for the lower.'

'What with? We've got no pegs.'

'That's all right; it's deciding where to place them takes the time. I'll get the system

17

organised now and it'll make the lower that much slicker when the stretcher does arrive. Since the chap on the top's dead—' Gareth had assured him of this, '—we'll use his stretcher for this one. They should reach us in half an hour.' It was a conservative estimate but by the time half an hour had gone by, another diversion could have presented itself to occupy Keith's mind.

'What about *him*?' The lad jerked his head, refusing to look at the casualty. The worst obvious wound, showing through the rent jeans, was a long gash in the calf; it looked as if a clumsy butcher had made a mistake in a leg of lamb.

'He'll keep. Just.' They were moving towards Lacewing. 'This is your worst one, you know,' Parry lied quietly.

'You can say that again! Oh, you mean I won't see anything worse than this—alive. Haven't you?'

'No.' He didn't say he'd seen worse dead.

'Do you get used to it? You don't feel anything?'

'I'm thinking about getting him down.'

'You're the lucky one. When you just take orders you've got time . . . But I wasn't *thinking*; it was the sight of him, of what they'd done to him.'

'They?'

'Rocks.'

'Yeah, rocks are harder than men.'

18

Keith sat down under Lacewing and, after spilling several matches, lit a cigarette. 'I'd like a drag before I start up,' he said superfluously and with an air of defiance.

Parry nodded companionably and squatted on his haunches. He picked a blade of grass and chewed it. Keith drew deep on his cigarette and watched the smoke dissolve. He was facing rightwards, away from the gully.

'Chaps couldn't do that,' he said. 'They'd stop before they got that far. Putting the boot in only means bruises, a cracked rib at best.'

'Not if they intend to kill,' Parry said.

They were quiet for a while, then Gareth came on the air to say that the stretcher was nearly at the top. He asked again if he shouldn't come down, roped. Parry refused. He didn't elaborate.

When he saw that Keith had stopped trembling he climbed to the Terrace, wondering why he'd found the delicate moves hard. It might have been because he was reversing them but he was inclined to think that the reason was he'd had no specific objective. For all he'd known he had been pottering aimlessly on an empty cliff; now he was acutely aware that this was the big one. They didn't come like this more than once in several years; some teams never got them. He grinned at the thought of the other two groups carrying boy soldiers for miles across the moors, and here they were, the Minera team: on the biggest cliff in the area

19

with a fractured spine *alive,* and nearly five hundred feet above the bottom. That 'nearly' saved them because the ropes were only five hundred feet long so he had a few feet of grace. Every facet of the situation was just within their limit and it made him feel good.

For the sake of Keith's composure he made a show of looking for the belay points but he knew where they were. He never forgot the techniques employed on a previous lower; he could have drawn a diagram of the anchorages and where he'd sited the men last time. He could use those same positions again even though the casualty was eighty feet below and off to one side. He explained it all to Keith who listened carefully, the shock fading before the technical interest.

The radio interrupted with Gareth coming through to say that the stretcher was ready to start down. Parry told them to go ahead and looked round for the best overhang to retreat under.

'That chap needs a hat now.' Keith motioned to the gully. 'Anything they knock down will fall on him.'

'I don't want to put a helmet on that head.'

They looked at each other, the lad anxious, his leader speculative.

'You want me to go down and shield him, like?' Keith asked. Parry nodded. 'All right. I don't mind. I might puke over him though.'

'You've got nothing left to bring up.'

20

'Lower me quick then. Don't tell 'em to stop the stretcher; I'll dodge the stones.'

'*I* can't,' Parry said, sorting the rope.

'You're the leader, Dad; it's not your job to be safe.'

'Where would you be without me?'

They grinned at each other, then Keith went over the edge on a tight rope and was down in two minutes flat. He shouted for slack as he moved along the ledge into the gully, then that he was in position. Keeping the rope taut, Parry returned to the overhang and settled down to wait.

*   *   *

Six men accompanied the stretcher to the Terrace. While four remained there to pull the ropes down and set them up again for the continuation down the cliff, Parry sent the others down Lacewing and into the gully, then followed, this time with one of the new arrivals giving him a top rope. There was no need to push his luck.

The casualty was in a coma and the others were as appalled as he'd expected them to be, not only by the boy's condition but at the prospect of handling him. There was a feeling that, like a piece of shattered china which by a miracle retained its shape, he would fall apart when touched.

Parry gave directions spiced with the quiet

coarse humour that would keep them going although he was privately deploring the situation: the ring bandage that he could only hope covered the depression in the skull because he was afraid to press on the bone, the terrible ease with which the flaccid legs went on the double splint, the need to pad the crutch particularly well because with this one surely no part remained undamaged. The jaw was bandaged and they manoeuvred him to the stretcher: amazingly straightened, incredibly still breathing. Parry hoped that meant they hadn't trapped the spinal cord.

He felt a wave of fatigue and stood up carefully, taking deep breaths. The blood beat in his ears. The others ignored him and continued methodically securing the patient on the stretcher. 'Watch those ribs,' he gasped. He'd forgotten to strap the ribs. If a lung had been pierced, surely there would be froth at the mouth? Too late now.

The sound of falling water soared and retreated at him from the well of the combe. He debated whether he should send someone else down with the stretcher; Keith had done the job before but only on exercise so he could use a real live experience, but now he seemed to be having difficulty in tying a bowline on the cross-member of the stretcher. 'Other way,' Parry murmured.

The lad looked up helplessly: the stricken look of one at the end of his tether. Parry stooped and elbowed him aside to tie the knot himself. Keith would have to stay on the Terrace.

*   *   *

The distance to be lowered was four hundred and ninety feet. He didn't have to use the radio much because the three lowerers were beautifully synchronised. He was proud of that but he didn't tell them so; it could have made them self-conscious. The stretcher was horizontal, going down parallel with the cliff and with a rope to either end. A third rope came to him. It was his job to stop the stretcher tilting, and to pull it out from the ledges; to keep it from jamming above the overhangs too and not to drop over them with a jerk that would almost certainly kill the casualty.

Stones came down. The shield protected the patient's head but not his body. They landed on the casualty bag with a dull thud but they'd padded him well; all the same, when one came down on the back of his own hand, Parry felt a measure of triumph, of balance restored. Now his hand bore a faint resemblance to the boy's, with blood oozing through the dirt. He knew a grim satisfaction.

It was lonely going down the long walls. On the biggest and barest: walking backwards down the rock, drawing the stretcher after him, with no discomfort and no strain, he felt as if he'd been doing this for ever, that he would go on doing it into eternity but that it was of no consequence. Emotion had atrophied. All he could hear was the tap of his boots on the wall. He was aware of the tight white rope running up into infinity from his harness, of the other lines to the stretcher, all taut as bow strings, and at the same time that he felt that the world held only one man who was totally alive, he knew himself a cog in a well-run machine. He was consumed by a quiet and overwhelming elation.

A shower of stones came down, shifted by a running rope. He didn't bother to dodge. Some glanced off his helmet, one, heavier than the rest, numbed his shoulder. Below him then he heard shouts, a grating and tumbling of scree. Astonished, he looked down and saw that he was only a hundred feet or so above the bottom and that the remainder of the team, the men he'd not seen since he left the summit, were there already, their faces turned towards him even as they scattered outwards to avoid the falling rocks.

He resumed his copybook posture grasping the side of the stretcher, aware of the metal hot and wet under his fingers, seeing a splinter projecting from a runner.

'Plane' and 'sandpaper' were words which floated to the surface of his mind while behind him, in silence, they waited to receive him.

CHAPTER TWO

They called Gareth Lloyd the Boy Scout, Scouts being synonymous in their eyes with 'rabbits': the term for anyone who was ineffectual on rock or, indeed, off it. They were indulgent towards him, suffering his background of village school and youth club because they needed him as a First Aider. He was a lanky man with a high forehead, warm brown eyes and buck teeth; not hard-looking nor hard-living, he stood out from the rest of them as an individual, a misfit, one who didn't conform. Even his clothes and equipment were different. Where the others favoured the latest Continental boots, a pair being provided for every member and the rejection of which Parry felt as a personal slur, Gareth wore old-fashioned clod-hoppers because, he said, they were more comfortable. He favoured drab anoraks instead of brilliant colours, and small rucksacks like those the youth hostellers carried on day trips. He didn't smoke, drink, nor, so far as Parry knew, watching suspiciously, have girls—although he seemed to make no effort to get too close to the men either. So far as sex went, he was a closed book, and Parry felt a patronising contempt for the man, but contempt tinged with awe when he observed the other's deftness with a broken body—awe and grudging envy. But the contempt was uppermost and it was galling to realise, as the team started down the screes, that since Gareth had been manning the radio on the summit, he must have relieved the operator of the set and assumed command. And, incomprehensibly, the men had let him do it.

Parry listened moodily as they followed the stretcher, the other briefing him succinctly on events during the cliff lower. It was borne in on him, with a trace of resentment, that while he had been guiding the stretcher down the cliff, the summit party had been getting on with their own work, sparing no thought for the dangerous operation in progress below. Well, good for them, he thought tiredly, but it would have been a different matter for Gareth if the job of supervision, which he'd appropriated so smoothly, had involved rock climbing. He grinned as he contemplated the reversal of positions: the First Aider forced to do what he, Parry, had done that morning. He remembered the top pitch of Lacewing and gave an angry snort of laughter. Gareth's eyebrows went up and he stopped talking.

'Go on,' Parry grunted, recovering himself.

A second stretcher had been brought to the summit by a scratch team of police and Army personnel led by Simon Massey, Parry's neighbour in Cwm Daron. Simon was a kind of author (by his own definition) but no climber,

26

nevertheless a powerful chap and one who, although refusing to be put on the strength of the team, would search and carry cheerfully when requested. It was logical that Gareth should send for him when a second stretcher was needed, but Parry was annoyed that the First Aider should have acted on his own initiative—and that, only for a corpse. Calling in extra men was the leader's job.

A minor irritant was the fact that at this moment Simon's party was ahead and might well commandeer the ambulance for their victim, leaving nothing but a Land Rover for the living casualty. It was the lack of trained personnel which bothered Parry; it was a long drive to the hospital and his men were not medical attendants. The boy might well die on them. Parry's eyes narrowed in appreciation; he would send Gareth as attendant.

They came to the lip of the upper combe and started down the headwall. From here they could distinguish the ambulance among the vehicles at the road-end in the bottom, and, a few hundred feet below them, Simon's party was straggling across the screes, looking, to the practised eye, a ragged and incompetent crew. Parry, who'd taken his place on the front of the stretcher when they reached the headwall, shouted for Keith and the lad came bounding down the slope as fresh and eager as a young goat now that he was no longer in direct contact with the casualty.

'Stop Simon and tell him to let us through. Then go on to Base and see that they have the ambulance ready to leave as soon as we get down. There's no time to waste with our chap, tell them.'

Their radio batteries had failed and even at this short distance they hadn't the power to contact Base.

'Will they take any notice of me?'

Parry opened his mouth to retort, and caught the gleam in the youngster's eye. 'Christ!' he said softly. 'Get away; let's see you move.'

He brooded over the figure dropping down the mountainside and reflected that, although he, the leader, had tremendous stamina compared with Keith's undeveloped power, at forty he'd never know again what it was to run with that careless speed and the suppleness of one who thought that broken ankles happened only to other people. His gaze wandered on. In the line of vehicles he saw the red flash of Ellis-Jones' Lotus. They had a good light for the cameras. He envisaged the scene as the television crew would be viewing it: rocks on the skyline gaunt in the sun's glare, Simon's party halted by Keith: a clustered group a little withdrawn from the body on the grass, Keith himself in the foreground coming like a bounding rock through the bracken and his hair flying—and in the rear: his own party winding steadily downwards and without haste, their burden the focal point of the exercise, the only bit that had been salvaged from the wreck.

Someone stumbled at the back. 'If you can't stand up, drop out,' he snapped, wondering if it were Gareth, unable to turn because of the restriction of the stretcher harness. 'Let's get a move on; you're going like a bunch of birds. This is a broken back, remember?'

'He's conscious,' came Gareth's voice, quietly.

They stopped and lowered the stretcher. Gareth knelt, his face in profile, showing his big teeth in a horsey grin at the boy whose eyes were open and urgent. Probably he wanted to urinate. Gareth asked him and the eyes merely looked hopeless, so he asked if the lad felt sick. The eyes didn't change but stared at the questioner with a look of desperate inquiry. 'Your dad is all right,' Gareth lied, and the eyes closed, satisfied. The First Aider pursed his lips and rearranged the casualty bag round the bandaged face with one hand, the other in the bag, on the pulse. His glance went to the valley, concerned and calculating. He stood up, resumed his place at the back of the stretcher and shook his head at the leader.

Parry moved back between the handles. 'Go like the clappers,' he ordered harshly.

Behind him Gareth said: 'It's all right, lad; we're nearly down. You can go to sleep now.'

Parry grimaced and his eyes were pained.

The carry was killing the boy. If only he would make the hospital alive it would be one for the record; the teams kept a tally of the victims they brought down alive but that meant hospital, not the road-end. It was a pernicious system because they might be alive when they were loaded into the ambulance but the journey to hospital was long, and with twisting lanes and bad surfaces the chances were that a casualty would be dead on arrival. Parry was pushing to get the unwritten rule altered: alive at the road-end should be the criterion.

The gradient eased and the path was turfy through chest-high bracken. Fragile harebells fringed the route like blue drops of dew. Here and there a bracken frond had turned yellow anticipating autumn but the hot breeze was redolent of recent heat waves: stale, as if the rocks were expiring. Parry's knees ached with the regular pace and the weight of his pack. The stretcher straps scraped his collar bones. He felt middle-aged.

'You're going too fast, man!'

'Let someone take over who can keep up.'

Silence, except for the soft thud of their boots, the creak of leather, an occasional gasp so low it might have been a sigh. He felt the stretcher tilt as two men changed places, then lift again.

The first party watched them approach. Most of them were sitting round the body, drawing on cigarettes, but Simon was standing, his eyes inquiring above the heavy beard. Parry shrugged at him, meaning the casualty might last, might not; his glance passed over the other stretcher, its burden sheeted and strapped with the face covered; what lay beneath looking surprisingly small for a human body, let alone an adult. He felt his belly contract.

People were floundering up the hill; he recognised a girl in a yellow mini-skirt and men in shoes and flared pants. Only Ellis-Jones, the television reporter, stepped neatly and carefully, looking for a good place to position his cameraman. Mollie Clarke of the *Express* stood square and solid beside the path, her hands plunged in the pockets of her old raincoat, hair like steel wool framing owl spectacles and inquisitive eyes. This was the awkward moment: the first impact. His cheek started to itch but he couldn't scratch it because his hands must be occupied with the stretcher handles. If anyone stumbled now . . . but Ellis-Jones had chosen his place: a gentle slope with the crags running up to a hard sky. It would make an impressive picture. The newspaper men had stopped a discreet distance behind the television crew.

'Good for you,' Mollie murmured, and his eyes met hers, momentarily and without expression, both aware that the camera was turning and all overt signs of emotion must be precluded.

31

Mollie lived in Minera, by choice and not necessity: a hard, sensational writer, geared to her market, and to the team which had become her protégé. Twelve years ago they'd caught her interest and retained it. She encouraged them, extolled, criticised; she was a self-appointed public relations officer. Respect was mutual and recognised and now, through the bustle and glamour of their return, with the media people pressing close, jockeying for pictures, what mattered most to him was the passionate interest in Mollie's eyes because this was the recognition that was most important. No one else could put gloss on a story as she could.

The small crowd of people round the vehicles moved aside for him. He slipped out of the harness and, leaving the others to transfer the casualty to the ambulance, he briefed the crew on the boy's condition.

The truck drew away and suddenly that part was over. His team mingled with the crowd and he had a vague impression of ladies in jumpers and skirts, of a trestle table incongruous on the grass and someone in a flowered apron like the one he'd given his mother just before she died. The women were tendering tea and cigarettes to the men like votive offerings.

He stood limply for a moment, alone, looking up the hill, seeing the second party winding down through the bracken past Mollie standing intent as an old heron watching the surface of a pond. A cup of tea was placed in his hands. 'You'll be needing this,' someone said respectfully as if afraid that it might annoy him to be disturbed. The Press, seeing him disengaged, moved in.

As he talked, he looked round for a face that might hold something more than familiarity, not knowing what he was looking for. He saw Keith. The lad had removed his shirt (it was unbearably stuffy in the valley bottom) and the tanned muscles gleamed with sweat. Aware of his leader's eyes on him, he grinned, showing the gap in front where he'd lost his teeth in a brawl at the Commercial Hotel. His lank hair clung to his shoulders and the pad of his crash hat had made a red mark on his forehead.

Parry was immensely tired and unable to view the scene as a whole but only as a collection of images. He started to let the Press do the talking, answering in monosyllables. He watched Mollie fall in behind the cortège, saw Simon approach on the front of the stretcher, like God in the old Testament, treading with a kind of slow anger, as they did with bodies. A girl leaned against the wing of a police car, apparently oblivious of the man at the wheel: a tall girl in faded jeans and blue shirt, with short thick hair cut to the shape of her head, and lazy eyes.

Mollie was coming towards him, flicking

pages in her notebook. 'How far had he fallen, Owen?'

'God!' The same question that everyone asked! Couldn't she wait?

'My dear!' She saw his expression and was stricken by her own clumsiness. 'You're buggered. Forget it—' she squeezed his elbow. 'Keep going for a little while longer; be pleasant to Ellis-Jones so you look good on the box.' She brought out her old hip flask and, unscrewing the top, splashed brandy in his tea. The other reporters moved away, searching for members of the team who would talk.

'Here, give over!' he exclaimed, laughing. He swallowed half the contents of the mug, tasting the brandy with relish. 'Mollie, I love you; I'll do anything for you.'

'You're all in and you'll do as I say,' she told him firmly but beaming. 'The booze will carry you through the telly bit, then you can get some sleep and I'll have the story off in good time yet, you'll see.'

'If I sleep now, I'll never wake.'

'Poor love, it must have been purgatory. Don't worry, everything's going to be all right.' She winked and lowered her voice. 'This is a great story, Owen: the best yet.'

He smiled; he knew that. He nodded towards the police car. 'Who's the girl?'

She glanced over her shoulder. 'Different, isn't she? I don't know if she's available. You can find out tomorrow: get her to help you sort the equipment it will be in a holy mess. She won't run away: she's staying at Hafod.'

'With Simon! He never said anything to me.'

'Why should he? That's his sister, Catrin.' He nodded, remembering that Simon had a half-sister. 'And why should he tell you?' Mollie went on. 'Perhaps he hoped you might be in the Alps or Scotland while she was visiting him. Being so much the elder he could feel a family responsibility—and you have the morals of a tom cat.' Her eyes glazed. 'Did I use "charisma" yet?'

'Just before Christmas you used it.' He drank the last of his tea and brandy. 'No—' as her hand went to her pocket, 'I've had enough for the moment; here comes Ellis.'

Ellis-Jones was surging forward, bearing the microphone like a sceptre, his cameraman bobbing anxiously in the rear. Ellis was a little red in the face and his beautiful silver sideboards had lost some of their sheen. They looked damp and scrubby and he kept smoothing them self-consciously but he was still jaunty if a trifle jaded. He'd been on duty since early yesterday morning, praying for something to happen.

Parry inhaled deeply, gave his empty mug to a hovering woman, and started to chat while the cameraman went into his excruciating crouch, circling for vantage. After a few responses he'd worked himself in, the camera started to turn and Ellis-Jones held up his thumb encouragingly.

As Parry talked he removed his helmet and exposed the short blond curls now dark and wet and plastered to his skull. He looked down at the hat absently, his face drawn with fatigue, but still talking with apparent compulsion (as they did after rescues) and talking well: describing the conditions, not emotively but as a record: the wind speed, the temperature, the fact that the cliff had been covered with that veneer of slime which made the operation so much more hazardous than usual: careful understatement which might mean little out of context but when the viewers started to think, the more intelligent of them, to realise that the cliff was vertical and the screes five hundred feet below where the injured boy had stopped, that he was shattered like a broken doll, they'd correlate—and as for the others, the dim ones, they could wait for Mollie's piece tomorrow morning when the whole scene would be focused for them . . .

As he talked he watched the girl with the short dark hair—Catrin, Mollie had said. She hadn't changed her position when the stretcher party approached and her glance at their burden was cool, incurious: so different from the usual spectators who would slink away, ostensibly horrified, to congregate at a distance and look back, because this was what they'd come for. Not this one. Now she moved, walking with a graceful step like a boy's, across to Simon who was talking to the police brass. The bearded man drew her forward to introduce her. The circle opened respectfully, imparting to the tableau an air of old-fashioned courtesy. She'd have been here for some time but no one spoke to her until they were introduced. The Masseys were class, the father a barrister in London. Keith was watching the group, not knowing who she was and fascinated by her reception. Keith was easily impressed.

'The responsibility of handling a damaged spine must be unbelievably onerous—' Parry's glance was dragged back to Ellis Jones, to catch the other's twinge of annoyance at his own word: wrong for the masses. The man went on smoothly: 'I wouldn't care for that kind of responsibility myself—' It was a cue.

'You've got to treat them like eggshell china,' he responded automatically.

'The sense of achievement: to get one down alive, after all this effort and danger, must be overwhelming.'

Parry realised, with surprise, that the other was labouring. He agreed, after hesitation, thus suggesting that this was a concept which so far hadn't occurred to him ('it's our job . . . someone has to do it'—playing the inarticulate peasant) but cursing Ellis because it was his, Parry's, business to introduce the achievement line, like a conjuror, with an air of astonishment as if he hadn't expected that one to emerge from the hat. Such a flash of inspiration should be associated with infinite weariness, implying that, in near-exhaustion, hidden springs welled to the surface. This time he'd missed his moment.

'This makes the eleventh this year,' he intoned. 'Three dead, eleven alive.' It sounded as dead as the corpses; he was sending good money after bad. They ploughed on.

'Would you say that mountain accidents were on the increase?' His back to the camera, Ellis glanced at his watch and mouthed an obscenity.

Parry allowed the anger to show but only a little. 'It's the parents I'm sorry for: imagine your boy walking over the edge—' the other dropped the microphone pettishly. Parry stared, realised that this could be taken for a sign of horror, and went on: 'My men aren't all that much older, you know; they've been out five times in five weeks—' the mike was presented to him again and Ellis listened absently, his eyes on movement beyond the rescuer's shoulder, '—operating in the dark, and twice in filthy weather. But then, gales are part of the job, an occupational hazard, you might say, and then a gale in the dark: it's better than daytime really, you can't see what's coming, only hear it, smashing down the rocks . . .' It was like a chat-show, it *was* a chat-show: the same things said each time, in different permutations. Ellis might remember what he'd said last time and warn him—like the boy walking over the edge; he'd used the phrase 'walking over the edge' a few weeks ago after a girl did just that in a hailstorm on Carnedd Iago. A few weeks back was too soon. Had it been months, repetition would have been immaterial; even climbers couldn't remember that far. But sometimes interviews came so fast he found it difficult to think of new things to say. Occasionally he'd have a striking idea, perhaps only a phrase, and he'd write it down to try to commit it to memory, like the one about 'wastage of human resources' although he'd got that from Simon originally. Ellis had sneered at him when he'd used it, told him to remember the level of intelligence of the public. They'd compromised on 'waste'.

The group about Simon was breaking up, the chief superintendent from Headquarters glancing uncertainly towards the team leader. Parry went on talking but without animation while the police dispersed purposefully towards their cars. Mollie approached Simon and conferred, the dark girl listening at first, then she turned and regarded Parry. The others looked across and smiled at him, Mollie nodding pleasantly. Gareth (who had not, after all, had to go to hospital with the boy) came over and waited, staring with vague interest at the back of Ellis-Jones' head, listening to Parry.

'. . . a wicked waste of resources,' he was reciting: 'human and material.' Even in his own ears his voice sounded flat and he didn't need to see Ellis' contempt to know that he'd made another mistake. Gareth's expression was one of alert curiosity now and it was to his First Aider that Parry spoke as the microphone was lowered in a final gesture of dismissal. 'I'm sick of the whole bloody business,' he ended coldly and walked past Ellis and Gareth and out of camera.

'Well, feller, they've been giving you a roasting,' Simon exclaimed, searching the other's face. Parry registered the sympathy but didn't comment. He was drained of words. He stared past his friend in a kind of angry boredom and caught the eyes of the girl.

'Come back to my place,' Simon was saying. 'Let your hair down. You look as if you've been fighting demons.'

'Don't we all?' He fidgeted with the buckle of his hat, vaguely surprised. 'It's all right on the hill, however bad it is. Things fit there, don't they? But nothing's so bad as when you get down.'

'For some,' Simon said, pushing him towards the cars.

CHAPTER THREE

He was not to get away as easily as that. Gareth had questions about the disposal of the body, and it was midday before Parry climbed wearily into his Land Rover to sit for a moment without the strength or the desire to drive away. His was the last vehicle to leave (like the captain and the sinking ship, he thought) and ahead of him the valley stretched, filled with a blue-green haze which was softening the sun's glare without reducing its heat. The breeze had died and the place appeared devoid of animal life. Even the sheep were invisible beneath the canopy of bracken. He glanced at the shelf for his cigarettes then remembered with surprise that it was eighteen months since he'd smoked. He started the engine and edged off the turf.

Simon's was the first cottage, its low rear wall and long roof turned uncompromisingly to the track. A flagged path ran under the gable end to a wicket gate at the front corner of the house and beyond this was an unkempt orchard and a fringe of rowans dripping scarlet berries above the river. The cottage itself had an air of casual charm, as if it did not set out to please and did so only incidentally.

Against its front wall and only roughly between the windows, sunflowers stood taller than the eaves (for the bedrooms were in the roof), and below the sunflowers, delphiniums and larkspur rose from straggling beds of marigolds. The blues and yellows, the late humming bees, the water beyond the wild garden, all this would have been gorgeous on its own but it was augmented by music—a horn and strings: a conversation between art and nature. He listened, leaning on the gate, and Mollie came out of the cottage, coatless in brown cords and a white shirt, bouncing slightly to the beat, carrying glasses and a bottle.

He opened the gate and followed her across the slabbed terrace to chairs half-hidden in the lank grass under the plum trees where she set down her burden on a white table stained with rust.

'Good,' she announced, perceiving him. 'You fixed it then? The body,' she added, as he looked blank.

'Gareth took it.'

'Alone?'

He slumped in a chair. 'He wouldn't mind. It's all the same to Gareth: alive or dead . . . dying . . .'

She glanced at him sharply and poured a generous measure of Scotch. 'Grape and grain,' she murmured, handing it to him. 'But knowing your capacity, you'd better not start on Simon's brandy before lunch.'

'What's that?' he asked shortly, gesturing to

the house 'The music?'

She listened as if she were hearing it for the first time. Her mood didn't seem wholly natural and he wondered if he were frightening her. She'd once told him that he was wild after rescues, but then everyone was a bit unbalanced for a while.

'A horn concerto by Mozart. Do you like it?'

'I wish I had a record player.' He was morose. 'I wish I had a lot of things.'

There was a pause. 'Such as?' she asked carefully.

He raised his eyes and brooded at her. Her expression remained neutral but politely expectant. He made a small gesture of helplessness. 'A stereo, a proper car—' he turned his head towards the house, 'drinks on the side, a variety, so that whoever comes, you've got the right drink for them; holidays—in the sun—' his eyes glazed, '—lazy holidays.'

'Alone?' Her voice was quiet but it dropped further: 'To get away on your own?'

'No.' It was even softer.

He drank his whisky deliberately, not tasting or sipping but drinking as if it were tea. He put the empty glass on the table and stretched his legs. His was an old cane chair lined with cushions. He felt his taut body relaxing and he tilted his face to the foliage above his head and closed his eyes. He heard the scrape of a match as Mollie lit a cigarette and he pictured her on the other side of the table, patient but alert, waiting on his pleasure. He smiled and opened his eyes and saw a blush creep over her tough plain face.

'Penny for 'em?' His eyes teased her.

'You're an attractive sod,' she told him with an air of defeat. 'I wish I were thirty years younger.'

'Thirty!'

'It would have to be that to keep up with you.'

Her eyes moved and he heard the grass swish but he didn't turn. The girl called Catrin placed dishes of nuts and olives on the table and addressed them in a voice which blended with the insects and the water.

'Can you restrain yourselves a little longer? Simon's doing *tournedos* but in a new sauce: something special with caramel which needs thought, and inspiration. At the moment he's contemplating. By the time we get to eat we'll all be drunk, which may be as well. Have you everything you need?'

Parry gave her a ritual hungry look and she smiled and went back to the cottage. She'd taken off her shoes and walked barefooted. He wondered that she wasn't afraid that she'd step on a piece of glass. When he turned to Mollie she was glancing through her notebook. He felt better now, not drained as he had been when he'd climbed into the Land Rover and had the ridiculous feeling that he'd been abandoned by the others. That was merely how it had appeared, because he was the last to leave; now he'd caught up with the people who mattered. He could stay here as long as he liked: drinking Simon's whisky, waiting for a meal that would be a bit weird but delicious despite its apéritifs of Scotch, talking to Mollie under the plum trees.

'Tired?' she asked without looking up.

'I wish it could stay like this. I didn't expect it: driving down the track, least of all this morning. What's that music they're playing now?'

'Vivaldi. What was your worst moment today, love?'

Her tone hadn't changed but he stiffened momentarily then relaxed. He slid lower in his chair, sipping his second whisky, remembering. Mollie waited patiently.

'There were several bad moments,' he began slowly. 'When the father told us that the lad had walked over the cliff—because that's what it amounted to . . . I thought he was dead then. He had to be dead.'

'But that would have made rescue more easy.' Her mind was sharp. Rescue was always harder when the victims were alive.

He agreed, seeing what she was after. 'There was another bad moment when I saw the tracks in the gully—but the worst time would have been when his hand moved.'

'His hand moved?'

'He'd fallen three hundred feet, he had a

45

fractured spine and he was alive—' her pencil traced quick spurts of shorthand, '—how could we get him on the stretcher without killing him?'

'No.' She was firm. 'I don't like that bit.' She cocked her head and stared at him thoughtfully but he was too tired to respond. Fatigue and elation followed each other like the trough and crest of one wave. To hell with whether she liked it; that was how it was.

'You needed to work out how many men you could get down the cliff,' she went on. 'How many of the team would be capable of that?'

'We had eight there—with Keith and me.'

'Enough?'

'It worked, didn't it?'

'Would it have been safer with more?'

'I hadn't got more.' Why was she antagonising him? He wondered irrelevantly what the temperature was. It was hot even in the shade.

'I suppose that the more men you have on the face, the more rocks they're likely to send down.'

'They do that anyway.' He wasn't listening properly.

She sighed. 'Is there a fine line between efficiency and danger: that you must have enough men to evacuate the casualty safely, but too many would jeopardise the whole operation?'

'Nothing's ever *safe*, only as safe as you can make it.' He grinned, thinking of Gareth, the Boy Scout. 'You can only have experts on the face. You leave the trainees and the non-climbers on the top. They have their uses; they had to go down the side and receive the stretcher at the bottom.' He was really referring to one man, not to the bulk of the team.

'Dogsbodies.'

'Don't quote me. Most of the team are unskilled labourers compared with the technicians.'

'That's nice: "technicians". Was it difficult reaching the casualty?'

'Nasty, very nasty.'

'Describe it.'

'A wall with incipient—with thin holds. A Severe.'

'Wait, love. Who knows what a "Severe" is?'

'A severe climb, and that means hard: a vertical wall with very small fingerholds; you've got to lean out to see the ones below and, because it's vertical, you've got to lean far out: from the tips of your fingers.' He paused, thinking, then smiled. 'All your concentration is in the top joints of your fingers.'

She stared at him doubtfully. 'That's a bit fancy. Surely, correctly speaking, your concentration would be focused on those holds which you were leaning out to see?'

'You can't explain to a non-climber,' he said

47

rudely. 'You hold your life in your fingers.'

She snorted coarsely and he glared at her in impotent anger. 'How about taking your life in your hands?' she asked.

'The whole bloody point is the holds are so tiny: they're for fingers, not hands.' He exhibited his own, like clutching claws. 'Don't you understand?'

She shrugged. 'A vertical wall,' she said flatly. 'With no holds—' He threw himself back in his chair, exasperated beyond belief. 'I've done this so many times, I'm drying up,' she grumbled. 'You're not being cooperative either.'

'I'm knackered. I'm getting old.'

'Hold up for a bit longer. This is what it's all about.' She gestured to her notebook, caught his look of doubt and took advantage of it. 'What's below this—severe wall?'

'Five hundred feet of air.'

'That's better—even though we must have said it scores of times. You can do it when you try, you see.' She was scribbling rapidly. 'Was it wet?'

'The rock was greasy, yes.' In fact it had been drying out when they came to descend Lacewing but no one could deny that there had been pockets of slime, and it had been impossible to dry their boots which were wet from the vegetation on the ledges.

'What did you think about?'

'Speed. He'd been there two nights.'

48

'But you didn't know he was there when you were climbing down originally, did you?'

He hesitated. 'You always gamble on them still being alive; that's why you take chances.'

Again she paused, concentrating less on what he'd said than on her own interpretations. 'All gamblers?' she mused. 'Or only you? Gareth, Keith, the others?'

'It's the leader takes the risks.'

'With other men's lives.'

They regarded each other warily, thinking of the printed word and the public. 'There's a point in time,' he acknowledged, 'when you have to take the decision to pull the team out. In winter, in a blizzard, this is easy because you bring them out before you see the weakest member start to suffer from exposure—and your object in doing it is to save them for the next day. All you need is acute observation: the ability to recognise the signs; you even know at which point you have to expect them. It comes with experience, even how to measure the gap between their level of resistance and your own—and that can be big: between the newest recruit and yourself.' He thought of Keith. 'It *can* be,' he repeated. 'But making that decision: to pull them out, in winter, is easy because there *are* signs; a time like today is harder, was harder. How far can you push them on a big cliff? You take the worst job yourself of course, that's nothing, but what do you let the second-best chap do, what do you stop him from doing? You know his level but *he* doesn't. And then there's the third, fourth, fifth, man: all descending grades, different standards of efficiency.'

'When do you decide the risks are unjustifiable?'

'I didn't.' He looked away. 'Have I ever?' he asked himself.

'You might have asked for another team to come up: to send down its best climbers.'

'*What* other team?' He was scathing. 'Come off it.'

She smiled indulgently and tried a new tack. 'So you brought the stretcher down—again.'

'I couldn't send anyone else. They were tired and shocked. I think Keith would have been all right once he'd gone over the edge but it was a very long lower—too long for his first effort—'

'And a fractured spine.'

'Yes. There's a knack to watching what's coming up at you and trying to avoid it before it gets too close. It had to be that way . . . it's not the worst job, you know, just the most dangerous.'

'So you'd call it the best.'

He smiled at her but said nothing. She went on: 'Do you ever think about your rope breaking as it runs over a rock?'

'Often.'

'And stones coming down—say, hitting your face?'

50

'No, you don't think about stones until they hit you, then your only concern is whether you can still function.'

'You must wash that hand.'

He looked at it ruefully. 'It'll hurt if I wash it. I don't like pain.'

'Don't give me that. Didn't it hurt at the time?'

'What hurt me was the worry that a bone might be broken. Then I couldn't have handled the stretcher.'

'How do you know that nothing's broken?'

'I can use the fingers.'

She shook her head in a travesty of awe. 'You're a hard man, Owen Parry.'

'It's just a job.'

'I've heard that before. Tell me what you thought about: going down the cliff with the stretcher.'

He sighed. 'Nothing.'

'Oh, try, for God's sake!'

'I didn't. I listened to his breathing and the sound of my feet on the rock. It was rather nice. I listened for the stones coming down . . .' His eyes focused on the mental picture that was still poignantly clear, on the recollection of the fantasy that he was the last man left alive.

'Go on,' she urged. 'Weren't you scared?'

'Not then.'

'When?'

'On Lacewing,' he murmured.

'On *what*?'

51

'The climb down to the gully. Don't put it in!' He reverted to the present and was pleading with her, watching her pencil anxiously.

'Why not?'

'The lads mustn't know.'

'It makes you human, Owen.'

'I don't want to be . . . The lads mustn't know. Cross it out, Mollie.'

'But it makes the whole thing more comprehensible to the masses. In the ordinary way you make courage look too easy. They think you're different because you're never frightened—'

'My God!'

'They do, I promise you.' She fixed him with her intent stare. 'Are you often frightened, Owen?'

He looked away. 'No.'

'Then say you were on this occasion.'

'*No!*'

Deliberately she drew a line through the last pencil strokes.

'It's the only way to hold the team together.' He was contrite.

'By pretending you're not like them.' It was a statement, not a question.

His mouth was a thin line.

'You rise in my estimation,' she said quietly. 'You've never talked like this before.'

'I haven't told you anything new.'

'Not much.' Her tone became business-like.

'Now let's have some background just for the record: why did he go down the wrong way?'

'In mist and at night? It's too easy for novices. He panicked: wanted to get help quickly when his old man collapsed. It might not have been dark then but remember what the weather was like on Friday evening. If the light was failing, and in that gale, anyone could go to pieces: inexperienced chaps, that is. It's as well the father's dead.'

'Owen!'

'I mean: he'd blame himself, wouldn't he?'

'But if he'd lived, and the boy lives, it would have been just a mistake, not a tragedy. With the team's involvement it would become a kind of heroic legend—' her eyes gleamed, '—at least, that's how we'd tell it—' then her face dropped. 'No sadness—except in so far as all heroism has some element of sadness in it.'

'Does it?' He was surprised.

She spread her hands. 'It's a fact. Heroes carry an atmosphere with them; I don't know what it is, can't identify it. What is sadness? Bereavement, loss?'

'You're being melodramatic. Whatever it is, there's none of it here. I'm bored, not sad.'

Perhaps she hadn't heard. 'The mother's at the hotel,' she went on absently, glancing at her notes. 'She'll want to see you, I expect.'

'She can see Gareth.'

Simon came out of the cottage and approached them, nursing his glass. He was wearing a butcher's apron but he was too large to look anything other than imposing. His eyes were bright.

'I need a break,' he announced, seating himself heavily. 'It's hot in that kitchen. The children are making some nauseating concoction with plums and cream.'

'Children?' Parry repeated stupidly.

Simon turned his slightly protuberant eyes on his guest. 'Catrin and Keith.'

'What's *he* doing here?'

The other looked at the glass in his big hand. 'He came. Perhaps someone invited him. Does it matter? He's Catrin's age group.' His gaze returned to the rescuer. 'They make one feel very old.'

Parry looked away, biting his lips. Simon went on: 'Sometimes I wish my father hadn't married twice or had sired more than one child by his first wife. There are nearly thirty years between Catrin and me, and all we have in common is a father and a certain similarity in superficial tastes. My mother was a horsey lady from the Shires but Catrin's is a beautiful Irish colleen; you see them in *Vogue* with Irish setters and a lot of emerald turf.' He was always verbose and a little pompous when drinking.

'Romantic?' Mollie asked, going along with him.

'No. just wild.' He roused himself and sat up. 'Have you finished cooking his hash,

54

Moll?' He jerked his head at Parry.

'The rest will come,' she told him composedly.

'Ha.' He looked at the other's hand. 'I take it no bones are broken.'

'No. I can move the fingers.'

'Lucky for you. Luckier than some.' Simon stared through the trunks of the trees towards the hills at the head of the valley. From somewhere, invisible, a buzzard mewed. 'At times like this,' the big man went on, 'one wonders why one is alive. If there is some power behind the scenes, on what principle does it select those who die and the ones who shall be left behind? One wonders (only when drunk, of course) whether death is ordained or totally random, not even natural selection. I would like to believe at least in biological selection: one can't live with no principles at all.'

'There's selection all right.' Parry was grim. 'They were complete novices: two generations of them—and they asked for it. Everything they did was wrong: not leaving word of where they were going, or rather, leaving it, then changing their minds, which was worse; not turning back when the weather worsened, being incapable in emergencies. They had no resources to fall back on, nothing.'

Simon regarded him morosely. 'I once walked off Conway quay when I was drunk. All I got was a wetting.'

'You were lucky,' Parry told him. 'There's no bad luck in mountains, only lack of judgement.'

'A hard man.' His host sighed. 'No compassion for human frailties.'

Parry glanced at Mollie but she was leaning back with her eyes closed, at least so far as he could see beyond the thick spectacles and the flickering shadows of the leaves.

'You can't have compassion on this job,' he said.

Simon's eyes opened wide. 'I believe you're right. You must be right. You have compassion, but you keep it in a box. You must have it, of course; you wouldn't be human otherwise.'

'Oh, I've got feelings,' Parry admitted off-handedly.

*   *   *

Discussion continued over the meal destroying Parry's last shreds of pleasure in the afternoon. Always on edge after a rescue, he found Catrin's conversation infuriating. They were like two electric currents sparking when they made contact. Keith exacerbated the situation by his obvious enjoyment when Parry clashed with the girl. The rescuer felt outclassed, sweating and elephantine in this sophisticated environment. He knew he was being dull and deplored it.

As they finished their *tournedos*, Catrin asked with some exasperation: 'Can't we forget about it? After all, there are plenty of people in the world; we can spare the incompetent ones.'

He saw this as a reflection on his job and denied it indignantly: 'The man might have been good at his work—and the boy, well—' he glanced at Keith, '—he was inexperienced. He could improve.'

'And yet,' Catrin added thoughtfully: 'It showed remarkable courage: going off like that to get help for his father.'

'Courage! It was bloody stupid. The sensible thing would have been to stay there and wait for rescue. By going off alone the boy made our job that much more difficult. They're criminally irresponsible!'

'Oh, quite,' Catrin said sweetly. 'But that's your *raison d'être*.'

'I beg your pardon?'

'Rescues are the reason you exist,' she elaborated. 'What would you do without them?'

'The accidents come first,' he countered, feeling boorish. 'The teams are formed to meet a demand.'

'But if the demand failed suddenly, if everyone like school teachers started to be careful instead of adventurous, you'd be out of a job.'

'That's right. While people are fallible—in

the hills—we're in business.'

'So your deploring their irresponsibility is hypocritical. You *need* victims.'

'Manners,' Simon remarked. Parry glanced at him carelessly. 'I can take care of myself. We're used to sniping by the uninitiated. The worst thing about it is the waste,' he went on airily. 'Of human resources.'

'How's that?' Catrin looked from him to her brother as if she guessed this one hadn't originated with Parry.

'Mountain accidents: the deaths and the rescues,' the leader said.

'There's no waste involved if they're stupid,' she pointed out. 'It's natural selection working in a sophisticated society.'

Mollie and Simon laughed, then Keith, sycophantically. Parry smiled with care.

'That's one of Owen's contentions,' Simon explained to his sister. 'Your minds appear to work the same way—fundamentally.'

She leaned back in her chair and regarded the rescuer thoughtfully. 'What is this other form of waste?' she asked: 'You said the deaths *and* the rescues.'

He hesitated and glanced at his host; he hadn't worked that one out—or he'd had too much to drink to deal with the niceties. His mind had gone blank in the face of the girl's hostile curiosity. After a long pause Simon said: 'On a big search there are hundreds of men spending time, energy and money, police,

58

hospital services, emergency telephone lines—
and all for perhaps one missing person only. Is
it worth it, even if he's found alive?'

'Perhaps,' Mollie put in unexpectedly, 'one
should do a cost-effectiveness study.'

Simon's eyes sparkled. 'You mean one
might decide how much energy to invest in a
programme according to the relative worth of
the product—i.e. the casualty?'

Parry said heavily, trying to apply the brake:
'It's bad enough when we have a Panel to run a
rescue. You're suggesting a study group to
decide whether there should be a rescue in the
first place.' He looked at Keith and detected
boredom there. He allowed a hint of sarcasm
to creep in: contempt for this pointless
conversation over the cheese and wine. 'I've
got enough bureaucrats on my back at the
moment, thank you.'

'There'd be no time for people to take the
decisions,' Catrin told him. 'In order to save
time, you'd employ a computer.'

'Perfect!' Simon exclaimed. 'That would
take the decision out of our hands. The great
disadvantage of human judgement is not only
that it's liable to error but that it's so easily
influenced by irrelevant factors.'

'So are computers,' Keith said boldly.

'Ah, but the incidence of mistakes would be
lower, dear boy.'

'And a computer wouldn't be influenced by
sentiment.' Catrin's eyes rested on the lad.

'You wouldn't be either,' she told him. 'This man would—' she indicated Parry with a nod. 'A computer would have no truck with romance and adventure—' she sounded stern, '—but there is the matter of potential. Now how would your computer measure that?'

'God!' Parry protested in disgust, but they ignored him and tossed the ball backwards and forwards while Keith watched, as fascinated as a kid at a wrestling match. Only half-listening to the exchange, contributing nothing, the leader felt that he had been relegated to the bottom of the class and excluded. Unlike Keith, he refused to show any appreciation for this slick performance. At last he was driven to interrupt.

'I'm only the guy who does the field work,' he told them. 'But I can see the point of this kind of thing: it works off the shock.'

'I'm not shocked,' Catrin said in surprise.

'Everyone is after a rescue where there's a fatality.' He was dogmatic and he envisaged no possibility of contradiction.

'But I had nothing to do with it,' she protested, laughing at him. 'You can't mean it's infectious—shock!'

'Well, that's simplification, but there was a strong atmosphere, even at Base, that you couldn't avoid feeling, and then you saw the body—' His voice died on the last word as he remembered that she hadn't reacted when she saw it.

'You're projecting,' she told him with the firmness of a school mistress. 'I'd have expected you to be more objective in this kind of job, although, on second thoughts I guess an objective rescuer wouldn't be efficient. He's got to be the supreme egotist.'

'How's that?' he asked belligerently, resenting her tone.

Mollie and Simon stared carefully at the table but Keith grinned openly. Catrin smiled.

'You do rather tend to lay down the law, don't you? People should leave word of where they're going, should turn back in a storm—'

'*Before* the storm.'

'—should be experienced. For God's sake, how do they *get* experience? But you're always right and all the others are wrong.'

'Not me,' he said. 'It's the rules.'

'What rules? Who made them?'

'Since climbing began over a century ago. The climbers made the rules.'

'They're imposed,' she said. 'It's a form of dictatorship.'

He relaxed extravagantly. 'I was afraid for a moment there you were going to say it was fascism.' His tone was patronising and to his delight he saw that it annoyed her.

'Safety rules are an intrusion on people's privacy,' she said hotly. 'I've a right to go where I choose in the hills, to change my mind, to come down where I like—without other people knowing.'

'Then you have a right to die alone,' he said softly and saw, with pleasure, that Keith approved the remark.

'That's what I'm saying.' Catrin recalled him with a jerk.

'How old are you?' he asked with feigned interest.

'Twenty-two.'

'You've got the death wish—like all the rest of them.' She stared at him in astonishment. 'We shall come out and rescue you, all the same; we won't hold it against you. We never do.' He allowed himself a smile of triumph.

'But then,' she pointed out earnestly, 'your injuries or even your death, lie at your own door, not mine. You've got freewill and a rescuer has to take the consequences, the same as everyone else; you can't slide out from under.'

In the heavy silence which followed Simon pushed his plate aside and picked up his wine glass. 'He was a school teacher,' he stated, with an air of changing the subject: 'Comprehensive.'

Parry looked at him with distaste. The meal had been heavy and rich and he shrank from the thought of the red wine and beef meeting all that whisky he'd drunk before lunch. Like the rest of him, his stomach was tired.

'I don't care what he was,' he said curtly. 'For me he was a body.'

Catrin remarked coolly: 'The Alps have

hidden advantages; you can roll a body into a crevasse on a deep glacier and leave it there.'

Keith gasped. 'Do they do that?'

Parry said coldly: 'They don't go to enormous trouble to retrieve bodies from crevasses, but they don't roll them in deliberately.' He looked at the girl without expression. 'No rescue team would do that.'

'Wouldn't you—in the Alps?'

'Of course not.'

'You're squeamish.'

Mollie said reasonably: 'The body's needed, isn't it? There's so much red tape nowadays. There's the inquest, and insurance; I should think those count more than the relatives who merely want to give the remains a decent burial.'

'Ridiculous,' Catrin said. 'All that bother. It makes good fertiliser too: a body.'

Parry was suddenly too warm, and with the sense of stuffiness, of being stifled, came the smell of ripe Stilton. He got up carefully and moved to the door, unable to excuse himself. As he stepped out on the terrace he heard low voices through the open window, curiously like angry parents:

'. . . unfair . . .' in a growl from Simon. Mollie: '. . . shouldn't have . . . been working his guts out . . .'

He heard Keith laugh and remembered acidly that the lad had been sick on Craig y Castell. That laugh was the final straw added to the load: the full stomach, the girl's teasing, his leaden fatigue. He went down the garden carefully, watching his feet and trying to close his throat. He stepped over the stile on the river bank, walked a few yards downstream until he was out of sight and sound of the cottage, then threw up in the water.

Afterwards he washed his face and, in doing so, reopened the gash on the back of his hand. He regarded the blood with morbid interest. It hurt. He sat down and, leaning against the eroded bank, allowed tears of reaction and physical weakness to run down his face. It had been a harrowing rescue, all things considered.

The water glittered hard in the light sifting through the leaves. He closed his eyes. If he concentrated, even on slight movements, he would have a headache.

He thought about Simon's cottage, but aspects which had pleased him earlier, now seemed without charm. The colours of the flowers were garish, the garden furniture shabby, the noise of the river monotonous; it was too hot. Cwm Daron was a backwater, an escapist's Paradise, and Simon was a drifter, a chap who couldn't make it in the outside world. Mollie was another failure; if she'd been any good she'd have been in Fleet Street long ago. She had no ambition and no application, just a flare for sensational stories. If she lost her job, she'd be nothing more than an old hag living on Social Security in a terraced house in a deprived area. She wasn't clever, nor even intelligent; she had never seemed so obtuse as she'd been today. Could that have been deliberate? Had she been needling him to make him say something indiscreet? He started trying to remember what he had said in the garden but an ominous twinge shot through his head like a bullet. He put his hand over his eyes and heard Keith's childish laugh as he'd left the table—not a sound which implied contempt for himself so much as admiration for the girl. Parry was defeated and his day had turned sour. He crept round the back of the cottage to his Land Rover and drove home.

CHAPTER FOUR

'What kind of insurance do you carry?' Meshach asked.

Parry put down his mug of tea and stared at his father: neat and respectable in his black suit, a picture in monochrome epitomising village life on Sunday afternoon. His tie and his shoes were black; the only colour about him was his brown face, grown lined and leathery in the quarries. Even his eyes were dark as jet under the low, bushy brows, but the hair was a soft white mane of which he was very vain. He washed it once a week with an alpine herb shampoo. What kind of insurance?

'The police arrange it,' Parry said. 'The chaps are ticked off by Gareth when a rescue starts and everyone on the list is automatically insured.'

'That's the team. What about your own personal insurance? You've got a policy, haven't you?'

He shrugged. 'Beryl knows all about it. I don't bother myself with that kind of thing.'

'You mean: you're not insured at all?' His father was spoiling for a fight: annoyed because Parry had spent the afternoon at Simon's instead of coming straight home. In fact, one of the reasons he had stayed out was in order to avoid his father. The old man never missed Sunday lunch at Dolwen. Parry buttered a scone thoughtfully, wondering why they could never meet without rubbing each other up the wrong way. The old chap was a reactionary; climbing for him was an English sport, pointless and dangerous, to be accepted or even ignored in his young days when only clergymen and university people did it, and that farther north on the big mountains, but now that it had become a popular fashion and attracted his son, it was anathema: a unique and useless occupation which brought in no money.

Beryl came in with more butter. The Parrys didn't have a refrigerator and food was kept in the dairy at the back. Her eyes observed the

66

table absently as she said, seating herself: 'We're with the Prudential, Dad; it's not much of a premium. Who are you with?'

Meshach ignored the question, designed to sidetrack him, although he addressed her: with gentle eyes and a tone like ice. 'I suppose that always having been independent, you're not worried about an accident and being left on your own.'

'Oh, I'm not independent,' she said lightly, accepting this not as a prognostication but as a move in the game they played most Sundays, and walking into the trap this time.

'If he contributes to the expenses now—' a very slight emphasis on the verb, '—the more reason why he should make some kind of provision against accident.' The tone changed, became sympathetic, at least ostensibly. 'Not that I'm suggesting you might fall, mind—' an absent glance towards Parry's bandaged hand, 'but it would safeguard her.' He looked at his son eagerly, as if diffident about interference when, in reality, he was seething with rage because Parry had been drinking and gossiping with his friends while Beryl—for whom Meshach had so soft a spot that Parry wondered if in the old man's mind she'd taken the place of his dead wife—Beryl entertained him on her own. Not that the old chap objected to that, he preferred it, but for his son to have been next door for hours without coming home was a fine justification for resentment.

'We're not frantic about security, Dad,' Beryl said, smiling gently.

'You've got to give some thought to it, girl, and climbing's not what you'd call a safe hobby now, is it?'

This got no rise out of Parry who was eating ravenously, hungry again since the loss of his lunch. He relished his wife's cooking: good, solid, starchy stuff, scones and two kinds of cake, and home-made jam with bread and butter cut thick.

'How is your book coming along?' Meshach asked politely.

Parry chewed phlegmatically, eyeing his father, his silence underlining the fact that he'd been brought up not to speak with his mouth full.

'Gareth was telling me,' Meshach went on, 'only twenty per cent of authors make five hundred a year. You've got to be good then, in the front rank, to make five hundred—what's that?—ten pound a week: less than my pension.'

Beryl leaned her chin on her hand, her elbow on the table. She regarded her father-in-law placidly as if admiring his appearance. Parry, observing this, remembered with a small shock that it was the way his mother had watched his father in her moments of leisure: with a kind of indulgent and amused affection. Meshach sighed and fired his last shot.

'The world's changed a lot since I was a boy—since *you* were.' He looked sternly at his son. 'Then no woman went out to work for the family unless her man was incapacitated.'

'We haven't got a family,' Parry reminded him, and looked meaningly at his wife. The old man was her pet: let her deal with him; after all, it was her problem. They'd been married for fourteen years and now, when it seemed too late, when it must be, she wouldn't adopt. Not that he wanted to adopt anyway, he wanted his own children. But Meshach thought something was better than nothing, so he was continually trying to persuade Beryl to consider adoption, using ploys which were quite transparent and which she resisted goodnaturedly but equally transparently.

'They're sending these little Irish children over for holidays again,' the old man pressed. 'Wouldn't you take one now, just for a week?'

'I'm working,' Beryl said. 'There'd be no one here; that wouldn't be a holiday for a child, would it?'

'You have holidays yourself, girl.'

'What kind of rest would that be for her: looking after someone else's brat?' Parry was indignant. 'And do you know what they're like: straight off Belfast council estates? They'd look fine in Cwm Daron: stoning the colonel's sheep and breaking his windows. God, we've got enough hooligans in Minera without importing them! Forget it, man; it would be

69

like taking a vicious dog and trying to train it to sheep when you never owned a dog before.'

'Kids isn't dogs.'

'No, dogs is more amenable. You give your mind to the parish, Dad, and leave us to get on with our own business.'

'I'm tired,' Beryl said quickly. 'The summer got me down a bit: all that heat.' She worked in a factory making protective clothing. 'Sunday afternoon's not a good time to discuss important things.'

'Sunday's a day of rest,' Meshach averred, turning to his son. 'She was doing the washing when I came. She cooked my dinner—which would have been yours too if you'd come home, and she's done all this baking, and ironed the wash while I had my nap in the garden.'

'Good for you.' Parry was deliberately casual.

'It was a fine drying day,' Beryl told the old man, apologising for desecrating the Sabbath.

Meshach left soon after that and she accompanied him. Parry was seldom home until late on Sunday, spending the day training with his team or, in the early evening, on stand-by waiting for accidents, but even when he was home he wouldn't walk down the combe with his father. It would have seemed out of place, although it was quite in order for Beryl to set the old man on his way.

'He's very proud of you really,' she said on

her return, hanging her coat on the back of the door and speaking as if she hadn't been away.

Parry ignored this. 'How far did you go with him?'

'To Bryn Mawr. The colonel asked about the rescue.'

'Was that all?' He was sardonic.

'He wanted to know when you're going to fence the river meadow.'

'Did you tell him I'd do it when I get time between rescues—and training—and mending the equipment?'

'He's worried about the lambs.'

'Hell, we're only in September! It's all of six months till lambing time. If Grainger paid decent wages he'd have had that field fenced last spring and those lambs wouldn't have been drowned. It was his own fault.'

'They rely on you,' Beryl reminded him. 'There's no money at Bryn Mawr to pay a contractor.'

'The Graingers had money when they owned the quarries; they should have held on to it.'

'For fifty years anyone who had money in the quarries was pouring it down the drain—' Her family had all been quarrying people, from the other side of Carnedd Iago. Her father and one of her uncles had died of pneumoconiosis.

'Exploiting the workers.' Parry mimicked his father.

'Not the colonel,' she said firmly. 'You never heard your father say anything against him; he's the only owner Meshach ever has a good word for. Incidentally, your father said he'd try to find someone to do the Bryn Mawr fences, so you can forget about them—'

'Who said to forget it? Not Grainger!'

'I said it. You *are* busy, I know that. And Meshach told Colonel Grainger that running the team was a fulltime job.'

'Did he!'

'He's proud of you, like I said; it's just that he doesn't understand.'

'But he's so stupid, he can't see farther than his nose. For Christ's sake, he'd understand if I was on a lifeboat, wouldn't he? Why, he talked all one Sunday afternoon about the coxswain at Moelfre after he'd seen him on the telly. You'd have thought that man was a cross between Lloyd George and God, and yet me! A hobby, he calls it. Does he think manning a lifeboat's a hobby?'

'It's been going on so long: shipwrecks, and people going out to rescue sailors. Mountain rescue is new; he just hasn't come round to it yet. He will, with time. Of course,' she added, 'it could make a difference—to Meshach— that the ships are necessary and climbing's just for fun.'

'*And* rescue?' he suggested with a threat in his voice.

'I'm trying to see how he thinks of it.' He

knew she was and he subsided. 'He's made a success of his life,' she went on thoughtfully. 'Manager of his section in the quarry, parish councillor . . . He knew there'd never be a chance for you in the quarries with the industry running down but I guess he thought, when you went away, that you'd land some white-collar job—' she smiled understandingly as Parry winced, remembering those years of wandering from job to job in the Midlands: salesman for a potato crisps firm, lorry driver, barman . . . He'd met Beryl when she was working as a children's nurse in Birmingham. They'd come back to Wales and, after another stint of bartending at the Commercial Hotel in Minera, he'd started the team: found his niche at last—but his father couldn't recognise the fact. Of course it was unpaid work, but it was work, and when his book was published—and went into paperback—then they'd be rolling in money.

'Parents always want to see their children do better than themselves,' Beryl was saying. 'He'd be pleased as punch if you were a teacher or in a bank—' Parry flinched, '—but rescue is too different. He can't place it in any category.'

'And it brings in no money.'

'Well, he's been poor. People think pay packets matter. I've tried to get it over to him that, outside of Minera, a lot of women work nowadays, but you know what he's like . . .

He's bewildered, poor old chap; the times have moved too fast for him. His arthritis is troubling him,' she added in parenthesis.

'Oh God, his arthritis too!'

Beryl sighed.

'And I suppose your feet are bothering you,' Parry said in despair. She suffered from bad feet and now she smiled a rueful acknowledgement. 'Everything's so bloody trivial—no, not your feet and the old man's arthritis—but Grainger's fencing and his paying miserable wages and who earns the money. All people think about is money.'

'You're worn out—and no wonder. Would you like a drop of brandy?'

He hesitated. He didn't really want a drink—never did after he'd been sick; what he wanted was for her to ask him how it had been on the hill. He needed to tell someone who wanted to know because they loved him, not because, like Mollie Clarke, they were thinking of hordes of faceless readers and how it would look in print tomorrow morning.

'I'm not a media man,' he said suddenly, taking the tumbler from his wife, wondering where she kept the brandy, and not for the first time. She'd gone out to the dairy for it.

She understood immediately. 'Several reporters phoned. I said I didn't know where you were.'

'Where were they ringing from?'

'London and Manchester. I didn't make a

note.'

'Lazy sods: trying to get a story long-distance. At least the chaps who come out on a rescue are doing it the hard way. Ellis looked exhausted today.'

'He's not a young man.'

After a pause Parry said: 'He's forty-five.'

'And putting on weight.'

He glanced down at his own flat belly, tasting the fire of brandy on his tongue. 'Simon's got his sister staying with him.'

'Oh, she's arrived?'

'Did he tell you she was coming?'

'Why not?'

'He didn't tell me.'

She shrugged. 'That could have been deliberate.'

He tried to look indignant. 'Just what are you suggesting?'

She was amused. 'You can't argue with your reputation. Shop-front, isn't it? You're tired; why don't you take the drink upstairs? I'll be up as soon as I've done the dishes and set the breakfast.'

'She's a tart,' he said.

Beryl paused in the act of clearing the table. 'Is she?'

'Keith's bowled over.'

'Oh.'

'It was too easy. She's a nymphomaniac: tight pants, thin shirt, bare feet: fairly gasping for it. She's rude too and Keith loves that.'

'How did Simon react?'

'He'd be annoyed; yes, he pulled her up: reminded her of her manners.'

'She was rude to you?'

'Taking the micky out of rescue! Would you believe it: a *girl*, jeering at us. She needs a good thrashing.'

'It's a pose, isn't it? The hard men not taking mountain rescue seriously because they don't want to admit they'll ever need it—'

'Who said that?'

She hesitated. 'Simon.'

'Yeah, that would be Simon; probably quite true too. Very likely. To recognise rescue as an essential service would be to admit their own fallibility.' He paused, savouring this, and his glance went to the chimney piece, searching for an old envelope but, seeing none, he gave up. It was too much trouble to write it down anyway. 'What's that got to do with his sister?' he asked: 'What hard men think about rescue?'

'She climbs.'

'Oh, yes? Walks uphill, I suppose you mean: a hiker or a youth hosteller. Only a novice could have made the kind of remarks she did about safety. You should have heard her—' He stopped and glared at the table, remembering.

Beryl smiled. 'Why should you be unique? I know rescue's your baby, and sacred, but sometimes I think that the more sacred

76

something is, the less likely the kids are to show any respect. I think they like to shock; that's why she'd be doing it: to create an impression. *You* haven't much respect for Meshach—well, you may have it, but you won't show it.'

'He's my *father!*'

'And this girl's young enough to be your daughter.'

His mouth dropped open then closed with a snap. She was right, but it made him more angry, not less. He was enraged by the thought that Catrin might regard him with the same amused indifference with which he treated his father's senile tantrums. Senility! He pictured the easy walk of her superimposed on an image of Keith surging through the bracken with his shoulders gleaming and the wind in his hair.

'I'm going to bed,' he said sulkily. 'Don't wake me in the morning; I'll sleep late.'

CHAPTER FIVE

He woke with swollen eyes and a bad taste in his mouth. The sun was high and the house empty; Beryl would have left for work long ago. For once he regretted his unconventional way of life which should have presented him with unlimited freedom but which, on a glorious morning, found him in an empty house in a nearly empty combe with nothing to do. Simon would be writing, or reading: compiling one of his clever reviews, or adding a few fine sentences to a short story; the Graingers would be pottering round their ramshackle farm and shabby house, and Parry: the Minera team leader, focus of all the rescue stories this Monday morning, was on his back in bed watching the flies on the ceiling and contemplating a free day in which he could either sort the equipment, tangled and filthy from the weekend, or mend the colonel's fences.

He got up and went downstairs. He viewed the set breakfast table, the bacon and eggs beside the cooker, the clean frying pan, with no slackening of resentment. They implied that he was incapable of the simplest actions; Beryl had to do everything for him.

The postman had been and there were two envelopes on the mat. One contained a glossy picture of a man on an ice wall in the Himalayas and, on the reverse, a form asking him to buy 'the greatest expedition book of all time' for £4.95. He looked critically at the photograph, trying to discover some detail which would show that it had been tilted, then he opened the other envelope.

Someone had had some thoughts on *The Psychology of Rescue* and had cyclostyled them. He read without interest as he ate his breakfast. It had all been said before. The author was a warden in a national park, and an exhibitionist. Parry thought of his own book and his advantages over an amateur. That brought him back to the realities of rescue and he felt a sudden overwhelming relief tinged with guilt that he hadn't been called out in the last twelve hours. He doubted if he could have responded yet again, and then reflected that he would have had no choice. Without him the team was a rudderless ship.

He rang the hospital and learned that the injured boy was still in a coma. Telephoning was merely a diversion. He looked at the brilliant sky beyond the window and thought that twenty years ago he'd have been on the hill by this time on a good morning. Ten years ago he could do two rescues on the trot without sleeping between them. Surely it was unusual for the body to deteriorate that quickly in a decade—or was it that the volume of work was increasing: that reserves weren't depleted but that more was now expected of him? It had been fine last night. He pictured the team with himself at its head, going fast up the headwall. They would have responded to another call—but how much could the heart take before it collapsed? Even quite young men had heart attacks. I must slow down, he thought; I'll have to stop drinking.

He left the cottage and, going out to his Land Rover, drove it round to the stone barn which housed the rescue equipment, backed, opened the rear door and stared miserably at the chaos revealed. He pulled out a rope and, with it, a sodden blanket, shreds of news paper, a wet and greasy sandwich. He sighed and started to unravel the rope.

The buzzards called clearly: a sound indicative of a windless day and rising thermals: Indian summer with the promise of winter not far behind. He liked winter, with the long snow slopes and ice in the gullies—if they were lucky—but he hated the end of summer. He felt at this moment, sorting equipment, that he was not merely wasting time but frittering away something that was infinitely precious and irrecoverable. Less than half a mile above him, under the soaring buzzards, the pale buttresses of Craig y Bera stood empty and beautiful above the trees. He leaned against the truck and stared at them speculatively, feeling the resentment and the tension recede to be replaced by a cool and specific desire.

*　　　*　　　*

In his position he could never approve of solitary climbing—not for anyone outside the tight circle of cliff rescuers. For the rock-climbing nucleus of the team the opposite prevailed; rescuers had to be trained for solo climbing because they seldom used a rope on

80

rescues. He didn't like it himself, not any longer; it was diabolically lonely and inherently dangerous. Except on rescues or training he climbed alone only after times of stress; he recognised this and wondered about it. He didn't want to climb *when* he was tense but afterwards or, more exactly: he would be tense, something would put him in mind of climbing, as now with the sun on a dry and empty face, and the tension would ebb as the new need flowed: the compulsion to be on the rock. It was curious that he should have to contrive a fresh challenge when he had so many problems already. There was his father's incomprehension of a whole way of life, incomprehension bordering on contempt, there was his lonely existence at home with Beryl at work all day so that he was forced to work in solitary confinement, whether it was maintaining the equipment, getting to grips with the paper work or writing his book. He'd once suggested to Simon that they should combine forces and work in the same house but the big man had declined firmly. If, as Simon maintained, a writer must have privacy, then he'd never produce a book. Mollie opposed this, citing the example of reporters who worked in crowds. Parry's book, she told him, should set out to be reports of rescues as he'd seen them, and the honest revelations of how he felt. The publisher's lawyers, she said, would take care of libel. He should write it how it was. She quoted Hemingway. He believed that he could write to this formula but it was no less distressing to go upstairs of an evening, to close the bedroom door and cross to the table in the corner and start to write in the lonely pool of light under the gooseneck lamp. He would sit there, imagining Beryl coming in to tell him to say goodnight to the children . . . and, at school: 'What does your dad do?' 'My dad's an author' or, more likely: 'My dad's Owen Parry.' Parry Rescue.

Why hadn't she had children? The doctor was supposed to have told her there was nothing wrong, but of course there must be. He was sorry for her; she wanted children, always knitting for other people's babies, but there it was: a big homely wife who liked kids and who was barren. He sighed heavily and almost turned back down the hillside because when he studied his own situation he didn't really want to do anything, even to climb. He clenched the fingers of one hand and opened them, staring absently at the rock above; surely, once he was up there, he'd stop being bored. At least, he thought with a grim smile, there'll be fear.

So he needed a hard route, something on which to stretch himself, something like Lacewing. What about Gazelle? His step faltered. Gazelle. It was extremely hard. The crux involved stepping across the top of a vertical depression where, two hundred feet below, any abandoned gear was framed in the walls of the trough. The move across the trough was just too long for a tall man's stride so, too far to straddle, the back foot must come off before the far side could be touched. Success depended on finding hidden handholds on the other side of the rift before one swayed backwards. Even safe in bed he would break out in a sweat when he remembered the hard move on Gazelle. He'd been taken up it once, and was terrified; only the rope had held him in balance as he groped for those hidden handholds. All the same, as a result of having done the route, his stock had risen with the team. He hadn't many good men at that time and the members saw little difference between leading a route and being pulled up it as second man.

To look at Gazelle now was a sick joke—but there were always miracles. He might experience that sudden surge of confidence that he used to feel in the old days when he could look at a hard move on a climb and know, not only that he could do it, but that he wanted to do it. There had been an affinity with the crux.

He paused when he came to the foot of the crag, feeling the waves of heat rise from his chest. Above him there was a sound like a stone moving: a buzzard landing perhaps, or a sheep trapped in a gully. Most of the rock was hidden now by the trees; only the chute of

Gazelle reared above him. It was curious that the more empty rock was, the more animate it appeared. He shuddered and started up Hornet: a climb of moderate difficulty some ten feet to the left.

Being low in the trees the initial rock was green with lichen but it was a popular route and the holds had been scraped clean. It wasn't a hard line; as its name implied, the sting was in the tail, and even that could be avoided.

He came out above the tree tops and saw the roof of Simon's cottage gleaming among its sycamores, and his own roof a few hundred yards downstream. As usual the combe appeared untenanted. There was no public footpath throughout its length. When the mist came down, odd walkers strayed this way, taking the wrong descent from the Skyline Route but, apart from traffic associated with rescues, only the residents used the glen. It was lonely in reality, not merely in his imagination: beautiful but a little too remote.

He went on for some distance then traversed right to come out at the crux of Gazelle. His immediate shocked reaction was that he was in the wrong place: to step across that yawning gap was impossible. He looked down and saw the flat triangular rock with the little marker cairn that said indubitably it was Gazelle. He stared at the other side of the trough in disbelief; he'd lurched across that himself—seven years ago and with a rope from above, but he'd done it. Now, contemplating it, he felt sick. He shook his head in bewilderment and turned away. Seven years. What had gone wrong?

There seemed no association between the two routes. Hornet was now a bore. He came to a grassy ledge, broad on the right, slimming down left to terminate in the middle of an unclimbed wall which plunged to overlapping slabs above the scree. A sloping crack ran leftwards up this wall from the end of the ledge. There were holds in the crack, large but at long intervals, and off-balance. The tendency was for the body to swing out of the crack and on to the wall.

He stepped off the ledge and into the crack. After a couple of moves he reached up for the next good hold and couldn't find it. He craned his neck, searching, and saw it farther away than he'd expected: a good eighteen inches out of reach. His feet weren't high enough. But how could he step higher when there was nothing for his hands? He wasn't happy about that left hand either. The bandage didn't interfere with the fingers, but now he wondered if a tendon might have been damaged. He thought he should jam the knuckles of his right hand in the back of the crack but it was sharply V-shaped and his fist wouldn't hold. He'd climbed this pitch innumerable times but for the first time in his career he couldn't remember how to make a move: how he was to get his feet higher when there was nothing for the hands. Then his foot slipped. He exhaled sharply and started to slide downwards, conscious all the time that the crack was leaning, that if he came out of it, even started to come out, his own weight would pull him sideways, on to the smooth wall.

He could picture his body leaving the crack, heard its soft and terrible crash on the slabs, the rolls and the slitherings, the final thud and the long silence, broken by the little stones and crumbs of earth which always followed a fall.

He felt solid ground under one boot and stepped back to the ledge. He walked a few yards, sat down with his back to the wall and dropped his head in his hands.

There was a sound like the friction of clothes on rock, something moved in the dead grass and a voice asked curiously: 'Are you all right?'

He lifted his head, blinking.

'You look shattered,' Catrin observed. She was wearing the same pants and shirt, but now she had a pair of lightweight climbing boots on her feet.

'Where have you come from?' he asked.

'Down the crack. What's more to the point: where do you think you're going?' He said nothing. She sighed. 'The rest of the climb's all right,' she said sternly, 'but you were asking for trouble attempting the top pitch with that hand.'

'You—saw—me?' It was difficult to get the words out with her standing there, against the light, watching him.

She shrugged. 'Let's get to the top.' She took a step towards the broad end of the ledge and the easy way to the top of the crag. He stood up and as he did so, feeling the ground under his feet again and his leg muscles hard, vitality seeped back.

'I'll have another go now,' he said airily.

She hesitated, her head on one side. A smile flickered at the corner of her lips. 'Go on,' she said goodhumouredly. 'I'll wait.'

He was so concerned with his own condition that the significance of her descending the crack hadn't penetrated his mind. All he was aware of was that she was either indulging him without realising the danger, or challenging him. If the latter, she was a monster, but he had to do it now, even if he fell.

He relaxed, not in confidence but in despair. The sweat dripped in his eyes, his hands were wet, but he wasn't afraid; he felt nothing. A few feet of struggling and it would be over.

He winced in agony as pain shot up his leg from ankle to hip. He must have sprained it unwittingly—or it could be hysterical (Simon talked about hysterical symptoms). He moved up painfully to the place where there were no more holds, thrust his right boot against the back of the V-shaped crack, then his fist, turning it, trying to jam it. Neither would hold, he was sure of that; neither could take his weight unless they were firmly wedged—and there was nothing to hold them in position. Struggling, using his shoulders, his buttocks, he gained a few inches of height, bearing down on the shaky boot, straining on the fist that moved in the polished V, then came out—and he was held by something invisible and miraculous under the boot: an incipient wrinkle perhaps. The boot moved. 'Oh, Christ!' he gasped: 'No—'

'Take your time,' Catrin's voice came quietly. 'There's a slit for your left hand; reach up and over your head.'

'God! Where?'

'Farther: another inch. You've got it.'

'That's not big enough!' He was indignant, angry with her for misleading him. But he could pull outwards on the slit, could with desperate strength raise himself enough to grasp a proper hold and muscle up on the last reserves of brute force.

The rest of the crack, now widened to a comparative staircase of good holds, was simple enough for him to climb slowly, collecting his wits so that when he reached the top he didn't fling himself on the grass as he would have liked to do, but sat down under control on a boulder, lacing his fingers between his thighs so that she wouldn't see their trembling. A spot of blood was widening on the bandage.

She had followed him up the crack without a sound. He'd known she was there only when he'd looked down for a moment and saw that, with one hand on the crucial hold, she was waiting politely for him to move up and out of her way.

Now she sat on the grass and after a while asked musingly: 'Do you still appreciate living in this combe, or has the novelty of it palled?'

He couldn't wrench himself away from his own thoughts to consider how he should answer. He tried to make the effort, failed, and maintained a surly silence. She glanced at him and again he was aware of that flicker of a smile, quickly suppressed, and eyes, not inquisitive as Mollie's were, but cool eyes holding no hint of sex—or did they? Intrigued, he returned her stare with deliberate insolence.

'For a man who preaches safety,' she observed, 'you have elastic ideas of your own limits.'

'Everyone has off-days.'

'It's a pity you didn't realise that before. I've never seen anyone closer to coming off the hard move.'

'That's not a hard move.' He was sneering at her.

'It shouldn't be.'

There was a long pause.

'I've led Hornet scores of times,' he boasted. 'I train my men on it.' She didn't respond. 'What excuse have *you* got for climbing solo?' He'd meant it to be flippant but it sounded dejected.

She sighed. 'The right to die alone—like you in that crack.'

'If I'd known you were on the cliff I wouldn't have come here. I never climb under solo climbers; they might fall on me.'

'I thought you'd come to join me,' she told him without coyness, merely stating a fact.

'I had no idea you were here; the trees hide most of the cliff, although—wait—I did hear a stone move. I thought it was a sheep or a bird.'

'A loose hold. I pushed it back in its slot. Perhaps I should have dropped it to confirm your theory that solo climbers are dangerous.'

'Where were you then?'

'On Gazelle.'

The silence lengthened until he asked carefully: 'You did all of it?'

'All? I started at the bottom.' She was puzzled.

'How did you cross the trough?'

'You jump it. There's a hidden handhold—'

'I know, I've done it.'

'Then you know how—' She stopped and considered him. '*You've* done it?'

'Yes.'

'You led it?'

'No-o.' He drew it out, his voice rising defiantly.

'How long ago?'

He squirmed. 'Seven years since.'

'Oh.'

'What do you mean: "Oh"?'

Her eyes wandered and then came back to him. She drew a deep breath. 'You've been living in a vacuum,' she said. 'I guessed a bit of it yesterday—after you'd gone home. They tried to impress on me that you were a great climber, but you hadn't talked like one: all that emphasis on safety. Besides, good climbers don't become rescuers; they haven't got time for it. I thought you were a fraud, that you'd been deceiving them deliberately—'

'You misunderstood,' he interrupted quickly. 'They were referring to me as a rescuer.'

'I don't think so.' She held his eye. 'You are the best climber in the district—must be—' she grinned impishly, '—or you'd have been toppled from your throne by now, but you've lost your sense of proportion. Difficulty's relative, isn't it? So because you're the best guy in your own circle, that makes you the hard man, but only locally. You've forgotten that there's a world outside with really fierce climbs and chaps who can do them. Are you trying to maintain the standard you were at when you were young?' she asked curiously.

'No. I was never any good. Seven years ago I

91

was pulled up Gazelle.'

'Why be so competitive about it? You know that the majority of people are rabbits and they stay at low standards all their lives, but they're quite happy there. There's some nice guys among them. Why not enjoy your climbing?'

'Would you enjoy doing easy routes?'

'What's "easy"? Depends on the climber, doesn't it? I have fun on my routes, but I'd be terrified on something above my limit. So there's no difference between us really; it's just that our limits come at different levels.'

'I see. You didn't feel intimidated on Gazelle?' She shook her head. 'But how in hell did you know there was a handhold to pull you round? If there hadn't been, you'd have come off; you know that, don't you?'

'I'd seen the guide book—and someone had told me there was a handhold; that it appeared when you wanted it . . .'

'You believed that?' She laughed at him. 'All right,' he muttered, 'I'm on a different plane from you—but for God's sake tell me how you felt when you came to that move? You didn't *know* you could do it. When I looked at it an hour ago, I thought it was impossible—and I'd done it!'

'I liked the look of it,' she said.

'Well,' he said resignedly, looking out across the combe : 'You're in a class beyond me—or what I've ever been. Hard man!' he snorted with derisive laughter. 'You're right; I got to believing what they said about me: the team, my friends, the Press. D'you know—' he turned to her quickly, glad to have discovered something in his favour, '—I tried to tell Mollie yesterday that I was frightened and she wouldn't believe me?' He looked away then, remembering that it hadn't been quite like that.

She regarded him with sympathy. 'I wouldn't have your job for the world. Now that's what I call dangerous: rescue.'

He managed a deprecating shrug. 'What I'm most scared of is making a wrong diagnosis and killing a chap.'

'You couldn't be blamed if you did.'

'I suppose not.'

'Is your hand all right?'

'Yeah, I can afford to lose a bit of blood.'

'You're interesting.' She got up, tilted his chin and kissed him. He was too astonished to move. She walked behind him and he felt her hands on his shoulders, close to his neck.

'Nice muscles,' she said.

He closed his eyes against a fog of sunshine while one hand played with his hair and the other slid inside his shirt to pull him against her thighs.

'You take a long time to get roused,' she told him, 'but you're all right.'

'Did someone suggest I wasn't?'

'Yes.'

93

He stood up, unable to control his feelings or his expression, avid to keep her eyes soft and laughing, even if she laughed at him rather than with him. It was his move but she forestalled him.

'Do you feel there's something missing?' she asked. 'There's no rope to coil.' Then, without a change in tone: 'We'll go to Hafod.'

'What about Simon?'

'He's out. He wouldn't mind anyway.'

'Suppose he comes back?'

'What a prude you are.'

He followed her down through the woods where sunshine flecked her hair with copper lights. His spirits fluctuated alarmingly. He was appalled by the difference between this one and the others: the girls who followed him expressionlessly from the Commercial bar to the back of the Land Rover. At the next moment his self-esteem took a turn: inspired by the incredible fact that he, Owen Parry, had met one of those hitherto unbelievable girls at the top of the climbing ladder and she had been attracted by him when she might have had her pick of the hard men—the real hard men. His eyes rested in amazement on her straight back and long legs; he observed that she moved with an enviable suppleness far superior to his own but most of all he was aware of her heedless air, an air which accepted himself, his present scrutiny and that shameful exhibition on the crag as if none of it mattered. If there was only one way in which he could redeem himself then he'd have to go through with it, although he would have much preferred to pretend he'd misunderstood her and, after one drink at Hafod, have gone home. But then she'd call him a prude again— or worse, and he'd taken enough knocks for one day. There was nothing left but to follow her.

CHAPTER SIX

'Who was it suggested that I might—?'

'Might what?'

'You said on the crag that— You implied that I might not want to go to bed with you.'

'Oh, yes; that was Simon. He's right, so far as it goes. You're a bit of a Puritan.'

To him one of her strangest attributes was that, like a very few men and no women except Mollie, she forced him to consider what she said. She made statements which appeared outrageous and which he intended to refute flatly but then he'd realise that what she said had the ring of truth. Now he said carelessly: 'Puritan is hardly the way my lads would put it . . .' meaning her to reveal the mistake which had caused her to think he wasn't a womaniser.

'People venerate statistics,' she observed, 'and your kind of reputation is built on them.

But the number of girls is irrelevant—and you don't need charm because the mountain rescue flash does all the charming. It's not the girls and the glamour, such as it is, but your own attitude that's important. Chaps can be obsessed by the idea of sex and make totally inadequate lovers. In fact,' she added thoughtfully, 'that's probably why they're inadequate.'

He moved his head on the pillow and stared at her.

'Not you,' she said. 'With you it's just a pose—sex.' She smiled. 'Are you integrated? Simon says your wife is placid and earthy. I must meet her. I suppose people settle down in middle age.'

'You get past it,' he agreed heavily.

'Not you, Parry.' But her tone was absent, like an automatic caress. 'I can hear a car coming; I'll go down and make some tea.'

He was thrown in a panic. She might not care that they had made love in her brother's double bed but Simon could take offence. The environment was all wrong; he had trespassed—and it was daylight. He'd always felt that the sex act belonged to the dark, particularly so in middle age; he was well aware that without his clothes the stringiness was starting to show in places. So Simon thought he was a Puritan, did he? With a reversal of feeling he decided he'd carry his boots downstairs; that should enlighten the big man. A rebuff for using the other's bed would be worth the expression on his friend's face when he realised that Parry had had his sister.

He waited a while, aware of a distant murmur of voices, then he dressed leisurely and went down the stone staircase in his socks to enter the living room at the same moment that Gareth Lloyd came in from the front door. Parry had no time to react before he was aware of Beryl standing motionless in the darkest corner, turned from examining Simon's books. There was a look of surprise on her face before she caught sight of the boots and then she stiffened. After a moment she smiled but her eyes were thoughtful. Parry had halted in the doorway at the foot of the stairs. He was astonished and frightened and he was watching for hysteria in Beryl's eyes. He realised he was holding his boots only because the First Aider was staring at them. He sat down on the sofa and started to put them on.

Simon came in the front door with a box of groceries; he glanced towards the living room from the tiny lobby, started to say: 'Make yourselves at—' saw Parry, checked, '—home,' he added in a different tone, then without expression: 'I'll be with you in a minute.'

He went in the kitchen. There was a tense silence which Gareth broke. 'Been climbing?' he asked.

'Yes,' Parry said quickly. 'We did Hornet, looked at Gazelle, pottered, that sort of thing.'

He glanced sideways at his wife and thought her lips moved. 'Been washing the grime off,' he explained, indicating his hands and then the stairs. Simon's bathroom was through his bedroom.

Beryl nodded. 'I believe Catrin's good.'

His head jerked involuntarily but her expression was open, not even curious. Gareth lowered himself into a deep chair and sighed. 'Tiring day,' he admitted as Parry turned to him. 'Lucky devil: climbing. Did you get the equipment sorted?'

Parry, who normally would have resented such a question from a team member, started to talk too rapidly about the state the equipment was in, and the report which he had yet to write. Beryl turned back to the bookcase. He wondered what she was doing here with Gareth but in the circumstances he didn't like to ask. Obviously Catrin hadn't known that Simon was bringing them back with him or she would have been filled with consternation when she heard his car.

At that moment she came in, carrying a teapot. Simon followed with a loaded tray.

'I expect we can all do with this,' the big man said facetiously. 'Been climbing, Owen? Oh, I'm sorry—Catrin, this is Gareth Lloyd: teacher, First Aid expert, youth club leader, not necessarily in that order. Probably the youth club's his main interest, isn't that so, Gareth?'

'It occupies me more,' the other agreed.

'There's rescue too,' Parry reminded them, gaining confidence now that he was sure the reason for his presence was going to be ignored.

'I forgot about rescue.' Simon handed cups round as Catrin poured the tea. 'So you were climbing with Catrin,' he remarked, holding the sugar bowl for Parry.

'On Craig y Bera.'

'What's she like?'

So she hadn't given him details. She'd had time while they were in the kitchen together.

'She's a hard man.' The mistake in gender was deliberate.

'I knew she'd spent a lot of time in the Alps.' Beryl smiled at the girl. 'I guessed you must be good.'

Parry realised that the women had met already, while he was lying in bed. He regarded them suspiciously, wondering what Catrin had said to his wife.

The girl said: 'I like climbing, that's all. Provided you're fit there's nothing more to it than absorbing what the fellows teach you to start with. You pick the best, of course.'

'Of course,' Simon echoed with heavy irony. 'Did it ever occur to you that for a girl to get her fill of climbing she must be beautiful or good (on rock, I mean; it's immaterial what she's like off it)? You have built-in advantages over the girls who can't afford to pick the best.'

'I'm not complaining,' she said easily. She turned to Gareth. 'Do you climb?'

'Up to Very Difficult; no more.'

'He's our First Aider,' Parry said. 'He doesn't have to climb.'

'What happens when a casualty is still on a cliff?'

'I've got a First Aid certificate too. I'm not so proficient as Gareth but I can manage.'

'You ought to have a First Aider who can climb to a decent standard,' she told him reprovingly while the others regarded her with surprise. 'Keith looks as if he'd make a nice climber—providing he can find someone to stretch him.' She smiled. 'He needs stretching, that one.'

'He'd be no good at First Aid,' Parry said shortly. 'On Craig y Castell yesterday—'

'He could get over that,' Gareth interrupted. 'It's like exposure in climbing: you work a nervous chap up by degrees. If you introduce him to very steep rock suddenly, then of course he's terrified. With chaps who don't like injuries you can get them accustomed if you do it in stages.'

Parry grimaced in disgust. Catrin looked interested. 'How do you do that?' she asked Gareth.

'Filthy pictures,' Simon told her. 'Technical books first with lots of colour photos, then slides brought along by a visiting pathologist, then the real thing—hot blood, as it were.'

'The reality is never so bad,' Gareth told her earnestly. 'On the hill you can turn aside and—'

She was staring at Parry whose mouth was open. 'Let's leave it till after tea, shall we?' she put in quickly.

'Oh, I'm sorry,' Gareth exclaimed. 'Certainly.' But he was looking at her, not at the team leader.

The silence stretched. Parry felt suddenly and inexpressibly depressed. He thought, with resentment, of the openings offered him this day which had promised excitement or at least an alleviation of his mood: the crag which had beckoned so beguilingly, Catrin's flattering interest. Both seemed empty gestures now which had merely increased his dejection.

'What's wrong with you?' Simon asked, with a rough edge in his tone which was alien to him.

'I must be a manic-depressive,' he answered helplessly, pleading for some kind of guidance.

'For God's sake!' the other protested.

Beryl said gently: 'It's been a disturbing weekend, Simon.'

'He's not usually as bad as this.' Simon tried to be jocular.

'I don't know why we do it,' Parry blurted, increasingly conscious that he was acting out of character, relinquishing his superiority.

'I've been wondering,' Catrin said thoughtfully. 'The answer: that someone has to

101

do it, doesn't seem enough. Does rescue lose its importance after a time?' She looked at Gareth who replied, as if Parry were absent: 'He's been doing it for twelve years. There's some element of shock after every fatality and perhaps the shocks are cumulative.'

'Do you really think that?' Parry asked in surprise.

'Mollie should be here,' Simon said. 'She'd talk about the need of society for heroes, particularly in a deprived area.'

'Good enough.' Catrin sounded doubtful. 'But that's only one of its effects: providing society with fixed points; it's not why chaps are drawn to it in the first place. Parry does it because he can't do anything else.' She ignored the leader's obvious anger and turned to Gareth. 'How about you?'

'We don't have a doctor on the strength and I'm the substitute. I meet the demand. As for Parry not being able to do anything else: you've twisted the truth. There's a niche and he fills it. Very few people could.'

'You haven't seen the papers today,' Beryl told her husband. 'I left them at home. They're pretty good this time. I expect you'll say they've made a lot of mistakes but they're full of praise for you—for the team. Mollie's piece is one of the best she's done.'

'She's got faith,' Parry said.

Catrin said firmly: 'The trouble with you is you're carrying too much responsibility. Why don't you spread the load: delegate? If there's no one who can take over from you now, why don't you train someone—at least train a guy to be a deputy leader: for emergencies, and to give you a break occasionally?'

'Who?'

The silence was broken by Simon. 'Who is the most experienced person after yourself?'

He shrugged. 'They're all hopeless.'

They protested, all except Catrin who studied him with interest. 'There's Keith,' she pointed out.

'Why do you harp on him? He's a kid.'

'He's the same age as me. You can see he'd make a climber, and if Gareth thinks he could be taught First Aid, what more do you want?'

'Nothing much.' Parry was sarcastic. 'Merely experience, and the ability to manage some of the roughest louts in Minera.'

She ignored this last. 'Why not joint leadership, then, like an expedition: Keith the climbing leader, and Gareth for the rest?'

She was advocating a change in leadership now, not merely a deputy leader. He waited for the others' protests on his behalf and when no one spoke, he glanced round them in bewilderment and saw that they were waiting for his reply. This was more than he'd bargained for; by indulging himself and favouring them with an indication of his mood, he'd been asking for encouragement, for an acknowledgement of the rigours of a rescuer's job; instead of that they'd taken him seriously, exploiting his honesty in confessing his own worthlessness. Now he had to find a way of slithering out of this ridiculous situation.

'It will take some time,' he said, looking pointedly at Gareth, wishing Keith were here to poke fun at the First Aider. 'Keith could be trained to a higher standard —and I agree, he'll make a good climber, but until he's had experience of hard—harder—routes, you'll have to go on the cliff—I mean, if you're going to relieve me of some of the work-load. You'd have to become one of the climbing nucleus; how do you feel about that?'

Before the other could reply, Catrin said calmly: 'I'm free; I could take both of them out while I'm here.'

Parry gaped at her. Simon said: 'Now there's an offer for you, Owen!'

Gareth grinned shyly, showing his teeth. 'I don't like to take up so much of your time, but it would be fun to be led up something rather harder than I'm used to.'

Parry said tensely: 'What standard do you think he ought to reach to be competent?'

It was only by an effort of will that he stopped himself wincing as she turned cool eyes on him. 'You've managed so far at a low standard,' she said. 'I should think if anyone can lead Very Severes, they should be competent on most cliffs. After all, you're not going to be asked to go on the big Snowdon faces; the professionals do those.'

His mouth opened, but to everyone's surprise, including his own, he giggled. He'd had a sudden fleeting vision of himself solo-ing down the fiercest cliff of them all. He hadn't even climbed on it. My life is a sham, he thought, and wondered how they would react if he said it. *She* would agree. He looked at them critically; the rest of them would hasten to assure him that he was doing a fine job of work . . . Gareth was protesting that Catrin would have some difficulty getting him to Very Severe standard—just as if he considered there might be some likelihood of it, when he'd never attempted anything harder than Very Difficult! She made a gesture of impatience.

'Look,' she told him, 'I've got nothing to do while I'm here; how about tomorrow?'

'For Heaven's sake, woman!' Simon exclaimed: 'He's teaching!'

She shrugged. 'I'd forgotten. I'll take Keith out tomorrow. Is that all right?' She glanced at Parry.

'He's working too.'

'He's only serving petrol at the garage; he can take the day off.'

'Cat, stop being so bloody domineering,' Simon laughed. 'You can't try to run people's lives like this.'

'Which is more important: the rescue team or serving petrol to tourists? He'd come like a shot if I asked him, and surely his employer won't mind. After all, he'd have to release him if there were a call-out, wouldn't he?'

'He can go,' Parry allowed judiciously. 'I'll ring Roberts at the garage, but if it's all the same to you, I'll come as well—as an observer.'

She nodded carelessly. 'I don't mind; it means three on the rope and we'll be a bit slow, but I see your point. Besides,' she added, 'you haven't seen me handle a rope; I expect I'll be a bit slap-dash for you.'

'In what way?'

'In the Alps one climbs fast rather than safely—I mean, the emphasis is on speed; you wouldn't be safe if you climbed slowly. So one's inclined to cut corners.'

'That's a bit like rescue,' he told her coldly. 'We break a few rules too: in the dark and in bad weather.'

'I'd forgotten that,' she said sincerely. He allowed himself a small smile but it was a meagre triumph.

*　　*　　*

Beryl and he walked home to Dolwen without speaking. As they approached the cottage he saw the Land Rover backed against the barn and remembered that all the valuable equipment had been left in the open for hours. As he followed Beryl into the living room he asked angrily: 'Why did you go up to Simon's?'

She looked bewildered. 'He gave me a lift home from the village and asked me to go to Hafod for a cup of tea. We stopped here first and you weren't about.'

'How did Gareth come to be with you?'

'Why, he was talking to me when Simon saw us in the high street; he wanted to see Simon about some business connected with the youth club. What's the matter?'

He flung himself in a chair.

'You're like an old bear today,' she went on. 'Has someone upset you?'

Was she referring to that moment when he appeared from Simon's bedroom? Her tone seemed too innocent. Didn't she *care*, or was she so dim that it hadn't occurred to her that a man didn't carry his boots on a visit to the bathroom? His depression deepened and he felt a compulsion to arouse some spark of feeling in her, even if it was hostility.

'I need a drink,' he said.

She went to the dresser and came back with the whisky bottle and glasses. His eyes brightened at the second glass. She didn't drink much—so she felt the need for it too. She poured the whisky without a word and, handing him his glass, sat opposite him, still in her coat.

'It's Catrin,' he began.

'I could see that.' Thwarted, he considered how to continue. 'If you didn't see her handling a rope,' Beryl said slowly, frowning as she worked it out, 'does that mean you were both climbing solo? You gave me the impression you'd done several climbs together.'

'Not together.' Realising she'd misunderstood his reference to Catrin, he regretted it, but recovered quickly. 'I did Hornet, she did Gazelle.'

'But Gazelle's the hard one that . . . Goodness, is she that good?' She stared at him, wide-eyed, increasing his resentment. 'I see,' she added softly.

'You don't see anything. I nearly came off Hornet.'

'I'm sure you didn't.'

'I tell you I thought I was off—twice. I forgot how to do it.' He debated whether to tell her that the girl had saved his life but reflected that this sounded too melodramatic. 'Why didn't you tell me she was a climber?'

'I did but you seemed to think I'd been misled.'

'I thought you were repeating gossip.'

'I was.'

He couldn't think of a retort.

'And then she—' Beryl stopped.

'She what?'

'You seduced her.'

'No: right the first time; she seduced me.'

'Why are you so angry?'

'You tell me.'

They stared at each other and for a moment he felt that they were united in a bond of helplessness: a flash of sincerity which was broken by his next words.

'You don't care, do you?'

'I care a lot.'

'Because she's young and attractive and a whore?'

'No. Because you're unhappy.'

'Oh. So if I'd come downstairs like a cat licking its whiskers and jeered at you and shown everyone I'd just got out of bed with her, you'd be pleased, would you?'

'It's yourself you're hurting, Owen.' When he said nothing, she added: 'I'd understand it better then.'

'Well, we'll leave it at that, shall we? You don't understand.'

'If that's how you want to leave it.'

It was like hitting a soft bag. 'I'm not going to stop seeing her,' he said, implying a threat, then, suspiciously: 'Do you want me to go on seeing her?'

She hesitated and looked away. 'I don't know.'

'The trouble with you is you've let yourself go,' he told her brutally. 'You don't even trouble to dress decently any more—' His eyes took in her shabby old coat and the worn shoes and he thought of his own flared pants, his new shirts. Goading himself he went on

'You never come out with me; your idea of a pleasant evening is to sit in front of the television with your knitting. You're always tired. The only time you go out is to the Women's Institute or to make tea for the youth club: old women and kids!' She wouldn't meet his eye. 'Kids,' he repeated viciously. 'It would have been different if you'd had children.'

She got up.

'Wouldn't it?' he said loudly, desperately, to her back. She didn't answer. 'Wouldn't it?' he shouted.

She went upstairs. After a while he drained his whisky and followed her. She was sitting on the edge of the bed, still wearing her coat. He stood in the doorway.

'I'm sorry, Beryl; I shouldn't have said that. I know it's not your fault.'

'Forget it, love.' Still she wouldn't look at him.

'Here,' he said gruffly, coming forward. 'Take your coat off. Look, I've brought your whisky. Drink it up; it'll do you good.'

When she did look at him he was startled by her expression. 'I believe you love me,' he said in wonder.

'Oh, my dear!' A tear slipped down her cheek. She opened her arms and he knelt and put his head in her lap. He felt her hands on his hair and was startled when he remembered it was the second time today that a woman had caressed him. 'Poor Owen,' she murmured. 'There now, forget it; none of it matters.'

She couldn't mean anything by it; they were

110

only the random words of comfort she would address to a hurt animal or a child. Neither words nor situation were unique; much as he deplored his wife and her shortcomings, he always came back, recognising in her a sanctuary which was as necessary to him as the things from which he fled.

CHAPTER SEVEN

'She solo-ed Gazelle!' Keith's voice was full of wonder. 'You're kidding.'

He'd appeared at Dolwen as Parry was finishing his breakfast. It was another glorious day.

'You don't know how the other half lives,' Parry told him, getting up and starting to clear the table. 'We don't *climb* in Minera; the hard men would call us scramblers.'

'Speak for yourself, Dad. Solo-ed Gazelle! Christ!'

'There's no difference in leading and solo-ing,' Parry said desperately. 'Except when you fall off—and the hard men don't think about falling; they're in a class by themselves.' It was essential to make this plain to Keith: to emphasise that she was in a different category from the team, and that included its leader. It didn't matter how far above them she appeared to be, so long as he and Keith were on the same level.

111

'I've never met a woman climber,' the lad confided as they went out to the Land Rover.

'Then it'll be an interesting experience for you. I climbed with a woman guide once: tough as nails; all they think about is the rock.'

'Not Catrin. Men come first.'

'She'll have a man when she wants one.' Parry hid his anger with an effort. 'But sex is just a side-issue with her: a quick poke and that's it.'

'How do you know?'

'That's my business. Here, coil this rope; we'll need two.'

'Hasn't she got her own rope then?'

'I haven't seen her use one yet. We'll take the gear. Women—'

He checked himself. He'd been about to say that women never possessed equipment but he reflected ruefully that this one probably had gear which he didn't know existed.

They walked to Hafod and found her washing the breakfast dishes with Simon.

'Where are we going?' Keith asked brightly.

'I thought Craig y Castell,' she said.

'You're the leader,' Parry told her heavily. 'Which route were you thinking of?'

She shrugged. 'I don't know the cliff. We'll leave it till we get there.'

On the approach he was subdued, deploring Keith's ingenuous questions but listening avidly to her answers. He learned that her father had been an active mountaineer in his youth, as were many of his friends; it was with their children that she'd learned to climb and with whom she'd done routes in the Alps: routes which were little more than names to Parry, but names wreathed in glory. This background, which she treated lightly, perhaps in order not to embarrass them, was strangely comforting to the team leader. There was an implication that anyone with the same advantages—of unlimited money, leisure and climbing companions—could have risen to similar heights or, if a man, even higher.

They sat on a flat rock at the foot of the screes and studied the lines of weakness above. The cliff faced east and the southern aspect of its buttresses was full in the sun. She said she liked climbing in the sun and he pointed out several severe routes but she looked bored and said idly: 'There's a line through those overhangs on the south buttress. What's that?'

'I don't know.' He was expressionless. 'It's not a route.'

'It's a good line. Has no one looked at it?'

'People have been here,' he admitted ambiguously. 'To the left of that,' he continued with more feeling, 'there's Fritillary: that long brown slab with the quartz streak diagonally across its top right-hand corner . . .'

She might have been listening but her eyes didn't follow his directions. His voice trailed away and after a few moments she blinked as if she were returning to them and looked thoughtfully at Keith. 'What have you done?'

He was startled. 'Me? Nothing much.'

'He's only beginning,' Parry put in quickly.

'He's got a nice build.' Her regard was calculating. Keith bit his lip and hunched his shoulders selfconsciously. 'You hear that?' he asked Parry on a high artificial note.

'What are you thinking of?' the older man asked, but he knew it was a superfluous question. Her eyes had returned to the unclimbed overhang.

'It doesn't look hard,' she mused. 'Not as far as the steep bit. There could be a stance just above it. There is one—of sorts; there could be a belay. You've got some pegs and a hammer?' He nodded wordlessly, cursing himself for bringing them. 'If you two change places below the overhang,' she went on, 'and Keith goes on the end: third man—' She stopped and looked at Parry conspiratorially. She meant that the two of them could get the lad up the overhang with a tight rope.

'I'm not being pulled up!' Keith was aggressive. 'I'm not coming if I can't get up under my own steam.'

'Sorry.' She did look apologetic. 'Perhaps we ought to do something else.'

She was rousing them. They all knew it. 'We can have a bash at it,' Parry said roughly. 'It's way above our standard, of course, but there's no reason why we can't get up with a top rope. The point is: how do *you* feel? You've got to

114

lead it; it's a fierce overhang.'

But he couldn't frighten her. 'You can't tell what it's like from here,' she told him reasonably. 'It's exposed but there could be good holds above the bulge.'

'There's more than one overhang,' he said frantically.

'No, they fine down to a point . . . you're not considering it objectively.' She stood up and her face was warm and excited. 'Come on, let's go and have a look at it.'

*　　　*　　　*

A long sequence of slabs and walls led to the overhang: airy, sustained, delicate. He would have enjoyed it if he hadn't been dreading the prospect ahead. Above him, beyond Keith, she moved up the face as if she had been reared in a vertical environment, and Keith romped behind her, silent with concentration while he climbed, breaking into excited exclamations when he joined her on the stances. Once, unable to bear the inanity of that distant conversation when he was on a thin move, he swore at them and told her to watch his rope. She was bringing him up, not Keith. She apologised and the ensuing silence was worse than the chatter.

He'd been in the vicinity of the overhang once before: seven years ago, when his leader (the same man as the one who had led him up

115

Gazelle) had made two attempts to surmount it and come away defeated. Now when he looked at it again, with those extra years of experience behind him, he was appalled. What was he doing in this place with a boy who was practically a novice and a young girl? He'd never done anything so hard. Gazelle? But that was on a minor crag and with a hard man—although he was coming to realise that his leader then had not been so hard as he'd thought, merely competent at a certain standard. This was a serious route on a big cliff: an unknown quantity (no guide book here with crucial information on hidden holds) and, in the event of emergency, there was no other party in the vicinity.

He was alone on a ledge, the doubled rope running through his gauntlets and out of sight round a corner. Keith had gone to join the leader. Just a couple of kids. He'd gone mad; what had possessed him to agree to this route? She would fall and he'd never be able to get Keith down these lower pitches, if he could reverse them himself: over five hundred feet of sustained climbing. He remembered that his whistle was in his other anorak, and that was at Dolwen. How long would he have to shout for help before anyone heard? Then it would be only hikers and what could they do in the way of rescue? She was going to kill herself, and wreck his career. He felt his body aching with tension and released his breath in a gasp.

There could be another facet to the situation. She was clearly good and had great confidence. Was he, in fact, just an old man being dragged up a climb as a favour? It was a degrading thought but more comfortable in the short term than the fear that the route was beyond her powers.

They assembled on a stance sixty feet below the overhang where they were so crowded as they tried to establish order from the confusion of ropes that they were constantly shoving each other inadvertently and he was furious in the face of her casual attitude to the drop. In the final pause while she studied the crux Keith said, 'Cheer up, Dad; it may never happen.'

'Ready?' Catrin asked.

She had conceded that Parry was the stronger second so now he paid out her rope. With her stepping on the slab, the fear dissolved in him and there was no more emotion, merely a climber going away and the rope running through his gloves. The only sound was the perlon scraping the leather palms and Keith breathing behind Parry's back.

The light was so good that every wrinkle on the rock was obvious. There weren't many. She used them as if they were proper holds, big as plates. He realised that she could retreat down this slab as easily as she was climbing it. He had never seen anyone move like this.

Irrelevantly, he wondered what Keith was thinking.

The slab steepened like a breaking wave, and above it the overhang stood in a petrified crest: not a big bulging nose but a kind of rock cornice. She would have to get her feet very high, with the bulge pushing her off, and then reach over the top. She wouldn't be able to make much advance the first time because she didn't know what handholds there were, and where; she'd have to go up, feel, retreat to good holds in order to rest. *What good holds?*

'She can rest anywhere,' he whispered.

'She's not tired,' Keith breathed in his ear.

She came up to the overhang so fast that he saw only the grand design and none of the detail. He was no longer a technician judging style but a man looking at a picture: a lay spectator. His eyes saw, his brain was asleep. Then she stopped.

She was stationary for a long time—or what was a long time for her. She was in a slight depression under the overhang which was about three feet above her head, like the jutting eaves of a roof. She moved again, bringing her feet high but keeping her hands low. Then one arm was extended and her hand explored the hidden rock. For a moment she was frozen in this awkward position, the legs crouched and cramped, arms and shoulders stretched and agonised. Then she retreated, bringing the upper hand down to its original hold. She started to peer and search below the overhang.

Parry could tell from the silence that Keith was holding his breath. Suddenly she turned and called happily: 'There's a nice hold here: in the back. Don't miss it.'

She went up again but now she had her left hand much higher so that her right could reach that much farther above the overhang. They saw the biceps harden and knew she'd found something—but now her body was arched like a bow, the rock forcing her shoulders back. Her position was a duplication of the overhang and awe-inspiring. The other hand came up to join the first: over the top—but now it was obvious that the strain was too much and something had to go. Parry's hands tightened on the rope. There was no point in warning Keith; he couldn't help. No one could. She was on her own.

One foot came off, gently, as if in slow motion, then the other. She couldn't hang there; it would be impossible for a man, and yet Parry was aware of no loss of control—on the contrary, he saw the strain leave the arched back as she straightened, or *seemed* to straighten; he had a momentary impression that her body achieved full stretch but since this was what he was expecting as a preliminary to the fall, it could have been an illusion. Reality was dynamic. One foot lifted easily, then the other, both finding purchase on rock at ninety degrees, the shoulders hunched, an arm reached forward: the body retracted like an organism which was more insect than human but as he gaped, asking himself how it had been done, his brain switched on again and informed him it was nothing more than a straight pull. But it had been a pull with nothing for the feet and the overhang pushing her off, and a drop of five hundred feet if she didn't make it.

She was moving out of sight, standing up. She waved and called with finality: 'Looking for a belay.'

'Oh,' Keith was murmuring, 'oh, oh, oh . . .'

'Piece of cake,' Parry spat out and, in the same tone: 'I'll come off; I'm too old.'

'Oh, Dad! That's climbing! Did you ever see anything like it?'

'Stop crowding me, for Christ's sake! I don't trust her with that belay. She's got to pull me up. Women! How will we know she's got the peg in firm?'

They could hear a hammer tapping. 'Listen!' Keith said. They were both listening hard.

The peg started to sing, the note mounting in a crescendo.

'That'll do.' Parry's lips were stretched and his eyes wild. 'Now she'll use the wrong knot.'

*   *   *

Keith went next. He took half an hour on what had taken her twenty minutes and only his youth gave him the stamina to stay in that place below the overhang for so long without falling. But by the time he decided to make the final move he'd lost a lot of strength. From sixty feet below Parry could hear his gasps, saw the top rope tighten and the lad's body draped on the overhang, his boots flailing for purchase. Then he was drawn up and out of sight.

Resignedly, Parry started to put himself in order. He knew there could be no hanging about for him. It was up to the roof and over at the first attempt, even with a pull. There was no alternative. She could never climb down it (he thought), and they had Keith as passenger. The third man had to join the others; they couldn't retreat to him. That was his last thought as he shouted that he was starting to climb and stepped off the ledge.

The slab was hard but by expending an inordinate amount of energy he got up it. He came to the overhang and willed himself to concentrate on the sequence of holds which she'd used. Exploring with his fingertips, he found the hold she'd mentioned and, as he'd suspected, it was no better than the inadequate slit which she'd pointed out to him yesterday on Hornet.

He warned her that he was climbing again and, by implication, that she might have to take his weight, thought that wasn't clear enough and shouted feelingly that he wasn't very heavy. 'Come off it,' she called cheerfully, and he pictured her glance at Keith. He hurled himself at the crux, reached the final handholds and found them good—but the strain on his arched back was excruciating, and his feet were slipping off those holds, now useless, below the eaves. He glanced up quickly, saw the clenched hands and the taut rope—the hot hard leader's eyes, and nodded.

Her outline stiffened, a pebble grated; he felt the constriction at his waist—but there was no strength left for co-operation. His feet were slipping.

'Pull, *please!*'

His body actually swung with the impetus as his feet came off and dropped, and then he was flat on his face, bundled somehow against her shins, and Keith was yelling with delight: 'Good for you, Dad! You've got some guts. I hope I can do that at forty—'

'Shut up,' Catrin said. 'And get these ropes out of my way. You talk too much. You're sitting on my boot,' she told Parry and pushed him away. 'It's a nice move, isn't it?'

* * *

They continued to the summit, Catrin climbing slowly and with care, almost languidly. She would have learned to do that in the Alps: to resume direction after the hard move with studied concentration, building up the reserves again because you never knew what secondary obstacles might be lying in wait after the crux.

They sprawled beside the cairn, finding comfortable rocks facing south, and she appeared uninterested in anything other than warmth. She hadn't bothered to unfasten the rope. Keith's eyes were closed but the older man guessed that he was far from sleep.

With an attempt at normality Parry reminded her that the climb must be christened, and she said in a desultory fashion that she had no gift and no interest that way. He suggested ridiculous things like Liberation and Boadicea. She wrinkled her nose but all she could suggest was South Buttress Direct. It was Keith who said, quietly and with his eyes still closed, like an old man pronouncing judgement, that there was only one name possible: The Cat, and they didn't contradict him.

They agreed to walk round the Skyline Route and, so far as Parry was concerned, the airy crest was a dream. She was careless, not of her feet but of her eyes and tongue. He realised now something of what the climb had meant to her; she had loosened up, and if she was still arrogant it was with an arrogance that included them. She was gay and provocative. More than once, while they waited for Keith to scramble up some pinnacle, Parry was racked with jealousy to see how she watched the lad. So when she looked down at Parry and said approvingly: 'I can't imagine you with long hair,' he was delighted that Keith should be within hearing. Moreover, the lad didn't like it; a boot banged on rock and if it wasn't a deliberate kick it showed that the other had been thrown off his stride.

From the last hill of the Skyline they looked down on Minera and the quarry levels. The village continued the levels in linear jumbles of terraced houses, and a film of smoke hung like gauze above the roofs.

'You'll go down from here,' Parry said as if idly, addressing Keith.

Catrin asked where he lived and the lad pointed to a cottage in the quarry. She turned to Parry. 'Will you take the ropes down?'

'Why, where are you going?'

She raised her eyebrows. 'To the village.' She added quickly: 'You've got a lot to carry; shall I take one rope and bring it to your place later?'

'I can manage; it's all downhill.' Dolwen was less than a mile away, in the opposite direction.

'I'll see you,' she told him pleasantly. 'Thanks for the climb; it was a lovely day.'

She turned, and Keith, after an amused glance at Parry, followed her jauntily. The older man stooped to pick up a rope, heard her murmur something and then the lad was calling back: 'Thanks for the climb, Dad.' It sounded careless and insulting.

He jolted angrily down the slope. All the pleasure: of achievement in a great new route (after all, he'd got up it), of the walk afterwards, of the sense of unity in the company which he'd felt once or twice, this evaporated before the feeling that he had been discarded; they'd gone off together leaving him to carry down the gear like an elderly porter.

CHAPTER EIGHT

On Tuesday Evenings Beryl had a meeting at the Women's Institute from which she went on to the youth club to help with refreshments. Gareth always brought her home. Parry heard her come in but he'd gone to bed and pretended to be asleep.

The following morning was dull and he knew before he drew the curtains that the weather had deteriorated. Even indoors there was a sticky feeling to the air. The cloud was down to two thousand feet but it wasn't raining. He brightened at this and thought that after breakfast he would go to Hafod and ask Catrin to take him up Gazelle. Then he remembered that the equipment was still in the back of the Land Rover unsorted, and this

125

was Wednesday. There was his report waiting to be written, too. He groaned. Normally he relished that kind of paper work but now he viewed it with distaste. Perhaps if he drafted it as he ate his breakfast he could finish it in an hour. It was now nine o'clock. He could clear the 'Rover quickly and still be at Hafod by eleven.

There were no letters. As he was cooking he heard Simon's car pass and he paused in the act of transferring bacon to his plate. Could Catrin have gone out with her brother? Hurriedly he cut two slices of bread, made a sandwich with the hot bacon and rushed outside.

He grimaced at the confusion in the back of the truck, reflected that he'd do the job this evening, the log report as well, and drove the short distance to Hafod. As he came through the wicket gate, he heard the sound of crockery being washed on the other side of the open window, and relaxed.

Simon was at the sink in his butcher's apron. Parry regarded him blankly. 'I thought I heard your car go down.'

'You did. Catrin's taken it.' The big man scrubbed intently at a plate.

'Is she coming back?'

'Tonight.'

There was a pause. 'Come in and have a coffee,' Simon said. Parry was still standing outside, talking through the window. 'Did you

126

want to see her?' the other asked carelessly.

'I thought she'd want to climb,' Parry said, entering the kitchen.

His friend continued to work at the sink. After a while he said: 'She's gone climbing.'

Parry sat at the table. 'Who with?'

'With Keith.'

Simon turned, drying his hands on a towel. He filled a kettle and flicked the switch, took a jar of coffee from the cupboard and two mugs. He placed them on the table and brought a bowl of brown sugar, regarded the sugar absently and pulled out a drawer in the table, looking for spoons.

'He's quite good,' Parry said heavily. 'Not in her class, of course, but he'll improve. He's the right age.'

Simon glanced at him. 'You didn't do so badly yourself, I hear.'

'We both had to be pulled up the crux.'

'She didn't say that.'

'Didn't she? I'm surprised. Perhaps she said we just needed a little assistance,' he ventured.

Simon sat down and regarded the other with sympathy. 'I'm ten years older than you. Forty's a bad time for a chap; he realises suddenly that it's middle-age. At thirty-nine he still thinks of himself as "in his thirties" and that's young. Forty is *significant.* You'll get over it. I did.'

'You always appeared so contented,' Parry observed in astonishment.

'I hid it, old chap. But then, the rat-race is a social ordeal as well as professional if you're in advertising. I was burned out at forty and positively welcomed middle-age. I didn't have to try any longer. To tell you the truth,' he added confidentially, 'I like being without love affairs; they're so wearing, particularly with the young and nubile dollies. I'm a lazy chap, really; you know that.'

'But you're not—you don't mean you don't . . . at all?'

'When the need arises,' the other assured him comfortably. 'But I'm pretty self-sufficient, what with the writing—and going on the hill, and a spot of visiting with the Graingers and Mollie. I find her as much stimulation as I care to manage nowadays.'

'What, sexually?'

'What a naïve chap you are, Owen! Mollie's been—well I wouldn't presume to say my mistress, but she's been a good companion for years, ever since I came to Minera.'

Parry gaped at him. 'Why don't you marry her?'

'There's no need to. We both like our privacy. Neither of us wants to live with the other; we're quite contented as we are.'

'You enjoy it that way?'

'That's what I'm saying.' The kettle boiled. When he'd made the coffee, Simon didn't resume where he'd left off, but asked after the boy they'd rescued from Craig y Castell.

'He's come out of the coma but he's not out of danger.' Parry had telephoned the hospital the previous night.

The other nodded. It was to be expected. 'Done the report?'

'No, I'll do it today. Where did they go, do you know?'

'I expect she's gone somewhere to find the sun.'

'That'll be the sea cliffs,' Parry said absently.

'Or Craig Dinas.' This was a low-lying crag which they used in bad or threatening weather. Parry thought that Simon knew where his sister had gone but wasn't going to tell him.

He stayed a further half hour ostensibly with the purpose of making notes concerning Simon's part in the weekend's rescue but in reality staving off the moment when he must go back to the cold squalor of his own cottage. In the end Simon was forced to drive him away: 'Must finish reading this book, my dear chap, I have to get the review in the post tonight: a hell of a chore, like your report. It's a dog's life, isn't it?'—urging the other towards the door so that he could return to his own interrupted—and enjoyable—work.

Parry drove back to Dolwen and set about the task of establishing some order in the rescue post, spinning out the time with small jobs like planing the runners of the stretcher, sweeping the barn, even oiling the hinges of the doors. Then he wrote the report and at two o'clock drove to the village to post it. On the way he called at the garage for petrol. Idris Roberts, the owner, was an overweight bear of a man, always disgruntled, an avowed pessimist. He had been doing his books when Parry arrived and, as he filled the tank of the Land Rover, stared at the rescuer gloomily over the top of his reading spectacles.

'You never said he'd be off for two days.'

'Young Keith?' Parry feigned surprise, glancing towards the repair shop as if he'd expected to see the lad there. 'What's happened to him?'

'Don't you know? You're his boss.'

'Only at weekends. He was out with me yesterday. When I asked you for him I said it was only for one day. Where can he be today then?'

'After a girl,' Roberts said, replacing the nozzle and squinting at the figures on the dial.

'I wouldn't stand for that.'

'Wouldn't you?'

'You've got to have discipline; you don't know where you are if he keeps taking time off without asking permission. If I were you I'd tell him tomorrow morning if he does it again you'll give him his cards. Tell him there's plenty of school-leavers around would be glad of a job serving petrol.'

'I want him tomorrow,' Roberts said. 'Suppose he doesn't come to work in the morning? Perhaps he thinks he's finished here,

130

that I won't have him back anyway.'

Parry looked grim. 'I'll see to that; he'll be in tomorrow morning, don't worry.'

The other nodded doubtfully, probably thinking that a school-leaver would be more amenable than Keith Williams who was starting to flex his muscles as a man.

Parry drove on, posted the report, and met Mollie Clarke coming out of the Post Office. He remembered to thank her for her piece in the *Express*. She beamed.

'Team work,' she informed him. 'Everything fitted this time: the weather, the rescue, the result: a fatality to make it serious and one survivor to give it the thrill you don't get with a corpse: the human touch. Everything was on our side.' Her smile faded as she regarded him. 'You look a bit under the weather, love; something bothering you?'

'Let's go and have a drink.'

She threw him a glance (he didn't usually drink at midday except immediately after rescues), but she went with him to the Commercial Hotel: a hideous place with iron tables and dark wooden settles and the decoration in shades of brown so that it was impossible to tell whether the ceiling had originally been white as one might expect or always the colour of smoked bacon rind.

'What's on your mind?' she asked as he set their drinks down. He'd chosen a table in the dimmest corner although the parlour was empty and the landlord was serving in the public bar.

When he didn't answer she groped in her handbag for cigarettes, made a business of lighting one and inhaled deeply, the movements slow and deliberate, giving him time. He sighed heavily. 'What do you think about adoption?'

She was startled, but only because she hadn't expected this particular subject, then she collected herself; everyone knew that Parry and Beryl would have liked a family.

'You've been discussing it with Beryl?' she asked carefully.

'Not discussed. We had a row. It was my fault.' His eyes abstracted, he reached for a cigarette from the packet on the table. Mollie's face, which had shown interest, lost some expression. He'd had a lot of stress during the last few months but it hadn't forced him to start smoking again.

'How does Beryl feel about it?'

He looked at her candidly. 'She'd do it for me, but that's not how I want it: I mean, she's going to have most of the work; I'd just have the pleasure.'

'And adopting only one baby doesn't seem fair on the child,' Mollie murmured. 'After all, you've got to think of the children as well.'

His eyes shifted and he drew on his cigarette. It made him feel drugged and faint; they said the first cigarette after a long

132

abstinence was nauseating.

'Did something happen to make this come up again?' Mollie asked. 'Adopting a baby?'

'Something,' he repeated gloomily. 'Everything.' She waited, deferring to him, sensing trouble. He ran his tongue along his lips. 'I don't know where to begin,' he muttered, staring at the empty fireplace. 'This must have been coming on for a long time: cumulative is the word—' he grinned without mirth and his eyes were tormented. 'What is it when you wake up one morning and you can put your finger on the cause of some trouble that's been bothering you for months—like a doctor coming up with a diagnosis?'

'You identified the trouble?'

He gave a bark of laughter. 'In a way—but I can't say that makes any improvement. You know how I've been living for the past twelve years: the team's been my whole life; there was nothing else—how could there be? I'd got no family; Beryl's self-sufficient with her job and her friends, she's even taken Meshach over as her family . . . But I had the team. Well, I've suddenly woken up to the fact that the whole thing's phoney: it's got no point.'

'What hasn't?'

'Rescue. I don't care about saving life; I'm not worried if they live or die or lie in a coma. Like Catrin said: we can spare the incompetents. But then if there's no point in rescue, you see, the team's just

133

supernumeraries. Now that's all right for the lads—they don't know, and since being in the team gets them off the streets, you might say rescue's a benefit to Minera. But what happens to me—the chap at the top—when the ground's cut away like this?'

Mollie said, as if she were exploring a strange country with her words: 'At the very worst you can be useful in leading the others.'

'Why? To help them help themselves? Because they're not in rescue as a service, don't believe that! Their motive for joining the team was to get in the limelight. Part of my job was to emphasise the glamour bit as the main incentive to recruitment. Once they'd joined and saw how it was, they couldn't resign because it would look as if I'd thrown them out or they couldn't make the grade. They were in a trap. We all are.'

'I don't see how rescue's a trap any more than life. We forge our own chains. What's rescue got to do with adoption, for Heaven's sake?'

'I used rescue in place of children: as a substitute, like frustrated old women keeping cats. Now I realise I've been exploiting a situation. I feel degraded.'

'How's that? If you'd been exploited by someone else, you might say that. But if you've just woken up to the fact that you've been twisting some situation to your own advantage, you're not to blame if you hadn't realised it.'

134

'I feel worthless. I was great, wasn't I: leader of the Minera team? So far as *they* know, I'm the same; only I know the structure was built on sand and the tide's come in and washed the sand away. There's only a shell left.'

She smiled tenderly. 'You're not unique. This is just disillusion you're on about.'

'It's more of a humiliation when the media have built you up. Footballers, pop singers—all the same: drugs, breakdowns, suicide.'

'They're unstable to start with—that type. You're stale, Owen; why don't you take a holiday?' When he didn't answer, she went on: 'You could go to Scotland.'

'The thought of my own company appals me.'

'Take someone with you.'

'I've gone past the idea of a holiday, Mollie; I've no interest in anything.' He grimaced with tension. 'I can't think of any reason why one should go on living.'

'For God's sake!'

'No, don't get me wrong; I didn't say I wanted to die but that I see no interest in remaining alive: I mean, why? Why do you go on living?'

'There's nothing to tempt me in the opposite direction,' she said firmly. 'I've got my work and friends, I enjoy myself; there are always challenges, in the long and short term. Of course,' she added with sympathy, 'Minera can be very depressing; as a villager you must

135

be affected by the atmosphere: the unemployment, the fact that so many of them are on some form of benefit.'

He brooded at her. 'Do you know what the suicide rate is locally?'

'No.'

'Do you think it's higher than elsewhere?'

She shrugged but didn't answer.

'And they all hang themselves,' he went on. 'Isn't that curious: the way we prefer death by the rope in this subject country?'

'Shut up, Owen! You've got no reason even to pretend you feel as bad as this.' His eyes narrowed and, staring at him a little wildly, she saw something there that made her pause and collect herself. 'I'm sorry,' she murmured. 'You've had just about as much as you can stand. What you need is some new faces. Look, we can't talk here; how about coming up to Simon's tonight? I'm going to talk seriously to you about the team; I've got a stake in it, you know, and I'm not having you undermining a structure that I had a hand in building. Now, you'll come to Hafod tonight?' He nodded. She squeezed his arm and stood up. When he looked at her he saw that she was already preoccupied with what she was going to say to Simon on the telephone.

He bought some cigarettes and left. It was turned three o'clock. Keith's mother should be home by now.

*　　　*　　　*

He parked the Land Rover outside the quarry gates and locked the doors. The village lads were well aware of the value of climbing equipment and that only a few pieces slipped in a pocket would find a ready market in any climbing pub on a Saturday night. With a bleak grin he reflected that petty theft of this kind was not necessarily confined to those outside the rescue circle. He might have given the team something to live for, but it was an extra incentive, not a substitute. Habit died hard with Minera men.

He passed through a gap in the crumbling wall and walked up a slope overgrown with thin grass and ragwort. On either side of the track ribbons of shredded plastic were caught on the thorn trees and his feet scrunched broken glass.

He came out above an enormous pit that had been used for tipping rubbish. Totally surrounded by chiselled cliffs, it was a gruesome place. When tipping had started, the rubbish floated, then it sank and absorbed the water until it was a level mass of mattresses and old oil drums with all the interstices filled by a conglomeration of muck in which two cars were trapped like ships in ice. Some years before an arm had been seen sticking up from between two mattresses. It was Keith's auntie: Bethan Jones, who had been strangled by her

137

lodger.

Parry walked past the pit, past stone piers and rusty towers rearing askew from bramble jungles. A drift of smoke crept through the scrub and he turned up a path to a cottage where a few hens were scratching in the yard.

Blodwen Williams came round a corner with an armful of logs. Keith's mother was small and thin with a nose like a beak and sparse hair that was too black to be natural. She was a woman who appeared permanently harassed: a martyr to her own anxieties and other people's demands. She'd left Minera when she was eighteen, to return two years later with a baby and a story of going into service with a company director, of marriage to a sailor and his desertion, but she remained Blodwen Williams although with the style of 'Mrs'.

In the kitchen she pushed the kettle on its gantry over the flames and looked more than usually disturbed as she waited for Parry to state his business. She would have felt that she was precipitating trouble had she inquired what was wrong.

Parry remarked lightly that he'd hoped to find Keith at home.

'He's at work,' Blodwen said, her frightened eyes showing that if she didn't know, now she guessed that he wasn't. The garage was on Parry's route from Cwm Daron to the village. Making it sound like an accusation, but

138

unintentionally, she added: 'He was out with you yesterday.'

'That was all right,' Parry told her. 'I rang Roberts and settled it with him, but there was never any suggestion that it should be for more than one day. I looked on yesterday as a favour. Keith's a promising lad; I wanted to see how he'd shape up on a big cliff.' It didn't matter that probably she knew her son had been on big faces before yesterday; she'd think she was misunderstanding details. People like Blodwen always blamed themselves if they didn't understand. 'I was thinking about some special training for him,' Parry went on.

'In the team?'

'Oh yes: upgrading him.' He looked out of the window absently, his slumped shoulders indicating that he could have made a mistake with Keith.

Blodwen was unable to control herself. 'Where is he then? Why isn't he at work?'

'I thought you'd know.' He turned to her. 'He could be climbing. I saw Mr Massey this morning; he hinted that Keith might be with his sister.'

'With Miss Massey! Never!'

Blodwen helped at Bryn Mawr, the Graingers' place. She might accept Keith's brawling in the Commercial Hotel or his putting a brick through the window of the Police Station but she couldn't accept the presumption of his being on equal terms with the colonel's class, even if Catrin Massey dressed more shabbily than girls in Minera. Parry wondered if Blodwen had actually met Catrin or merely heard gossip.

'I was talking to Roberts,' he told her. 'I'm afraid Keith will be given his cards if he doesn't go to work tomorrow morning. I'm involved myself because I doubt very much that he'll find another job in the village if he loses that one. He's had a few, hasn't he?'

She stared at him. 'There's no work,' she murmured, and then, betraying herself: 'And he doesn't like what there is, except the garage. The colonel was wanting him to fence the lambing fields, but Keith says he don't pay enough.'

'Colonel Grainger's not a rich man,' Parry said firmly, 'but he's still got a lot of influence, being a magistrate. He's given Keith a few chances in his time; he'll be upset if he's sacked from the garage.'

'Oh, he won't be! He loves working in the repair shop. I'll speak to him tonight, as soon as he gets in; it's only a temporary thing, I'm sure, he'll have been knocked off his feet by her. You know what young girls are like these days: after anything in trousers; not that my boy isn't a fine lad, he could take his pick of girls in Minera if he'd a mind—and probably does, although he'll not let on to me—but Miss Massey, no, that's going too far.' She was silent, pondering perhaps why Catrin Massey wasn't right for her boy, then she returned to more familiar topics. 'We need the money too; I'll tell him that. There's my pay but that's not much. Mind you, if I went to work for the Commercial, I'd get more than I do at Bryn Mawr, but the hotels is seasonal and Mrs Grainger wouldn't take me back. Any road, she'd have someone else by then. So I got to stay at Bryn Mawr, see? I don't want Keith upsetting the colonel.'

'You keep this place very nice,' Parry said, approving the black-leaded range. 'The Graingers are lucky to have you.'

She gave a quick bewildered smile, then assumed her habitual mask of distress. 'He'll listen to me,' she said, but without conviction.

'It might come better from you than from me,' Parry suggested. 'Climbing together, we treat each other like equals: equal ages, I mean; he might resent it if he knew I'd come to see you.'

'I won't say anything.'

'How would you know about him not being at work?'

'The colonel could have told me. If he'd called for petrol, he'd have known.'

'Yes.' He went on thoughtfully. 'I wouldn't want him to leave the village; I was getting to depend on him: young, enthusiastic, a beautiful climber. I have to train someone to take over from me some time.'

'Keith! Leader of the team! You don't mean

it!'

'Someone has to be.' He smiled ruefully, taking her into his confidence. 'It would take a while. I don't say he'll do, mind; I said I was considering it. There are others have been in the team much longer but—Keith's got something . . . He's only a lad but I think one day he'll be able to handle men.'

'Keith!' She regarded him with awe but not disbelief. She was a simple soul.

'It's a matter of ability—and of potential,' he told her earnestly. 'It's with his technique that he shows most promise. The team respects someone who's superior to them: who can do everything better. In a few years' time they'll be eating out of his hand.'

Her eyes were brimming with tears. She didn't say anything but set about making the tea. 'Mind you,' Parry said sternly to her back, 'I don't think he should know we've been talking about him.'

'I won't breathe a word; that wouldn't be right.' No, Parry was the superior and only he could take the initiative with Keith at least in this matter. Blodwen's job was to keep him at work. She came close to Parry. 'It won't be dangerous, will it: him being the leader?'

'Bless you!' He stood up and put an arm round her thin shoulders. With a shock he realised that this drab old woman was the same age as himself. 'That's all a lot of bull: the danger—just something the papers dream up. It's sensational: with the team all over the front pages after a good rescue, and on the telly—' he meant Keith's picture, of course, and he saw by her wide eyes that she was seeing it too, '—but it's not dangerous. We risk our reputations, not our necks. It's a glamour racket: rescue, that's all.'

'If he lost his job—' she began sadly.

'Then he'd have to leave us.' Parry was brisk. 'I'm not having any layabouts in my team; we're too much in the public eye.'

CHAPTER NINE

Although it was only four-thirty and Beryl didn't finish until five, he drove to the factory where she worked. As he'd expected, word of his appearance reached her almost immediately and he had only a moment to wait before she came across the car park. He regarded her haggardly.

'I don't mind waiting.' He was justifying his presence. 'It's not worth going back to the combe without picking you up first.'

She didn't ask where he'd been. 'Well, if you don't mind waiting . . . Maybe I can get away a few minutes early . . .'

'Don't trouble. By the way, we're invited to Simon's tonight.'

'Oh, yes?' She looked at him sharply,

guessing the remark had some significance and wondering what it was. 'I'm invited too?' she asked, probing.

His eyes widened. 'You don't feel up to it?' He sounded concerned.

'His parties are a bit . . .'

'A bit what?'

'Lively.' She looked away. 'Sophisticated. You need to be ready for them.' She smiled wryly. 'I don't feel like one of Simon's parties tonight.'

'That's all right. You don't mind—?'

'No, you go. I'll stay in the village; there's someone I want to see this evening—one of the girls.'

His hand moved to the ignition. 'How will you get home?'

'Her husband will run me as far as the combe. I'll be all right.'

He drove down the main valley. Going through the chestnut woods below the last of the tips, something dark flickered across a corner of his vision and he braked with a start. Behind him there was a squeal of sliding rubber. He accelerated in a cold sweat and the following car came out in an angry swerve on one long blare of horn. Parry would have liked the chap to stop for a confrontation, verbal or physical, but evidently the rescue signs on the 'Rover were a deterrent; the car vanished round the next bend.

He turned on the minor road that crossed

144

the valley, then right again on the Cwm Daron track. Ahead lay the opening of the combe with nothing visible of the skyline because the cloud was down to a thousand feet, and dropping. Soon the combe itself would be full of mist and as he drove up the stony gradient under the rhododendrons of Bryn Mawr, the first drops of rain showed on the windscreen. It was setting in for a wet night. He wondered if Catrin were home yet.

He parked the Land Rover and let himself into the cottage, frowning even before he saw the cleared and empty table, the dead grate, the total absence of humanity. The silence too, was dead. He switched on the transistor and winced at a frenetic blast of sound. He turned down the volume until the pop was a background murmur and looked round for something to do.

Simon liked routine and in the normal way the big man would eat at seven so, since Parry had been invited to Hafod only to drink, he had upwards of two hours to kill. He reflected that Simon might not have agreed to a party; he tried to imagine the other's reaction to Mollie's telephone call (she must have phoned when she left the Commercial). If he wanted to work he might have refused, but if Catrin were home, would he work in the evening? Where were Keith and Catrin at this moment?

He lit a cigarette and prowled to the window. The cloud was tangled in the tops of the trees on the farther slope. The evenings were drawing in. It would be dark early tonight.

He went to the dresser cupboard and poured himself a whisky. He wondered how he could have enjoyed his Scotch over the last eighteen months without a cigarette to accompany it. It was comforting to see the smoke in the room: something moving other than himself. They didn't have a dog because it was sheep country and he wouldn't keep a dog tied up all day. He wondered how other people coped with empty homes.

The cloud descended and the rain increased. It could have been worse; there was no wind and the rain fell straight and solid. It was the kind of night they didn't much mind going out providing the rescue was simple: a body to be retrieved from the foot of a cliff, or someone collapsed at a specific point on a path. He didn't think the rain would continue for long; it was too heavy. There was a tightness inside his skull: not painful, merely a suggestion of constriction; there could be thunder about.

After his second whisky aggression replaced diffidence and he rang Simon. They'd eaten already, the other said; he should come straight up.

The rain beat on his hood and the track was a running stream. On the bank tree trunks gleamed in the light of his torch. The smells

146

were clean and earthy with a tang of woodsmoke. When he came to a gateway in the wall he stopped and switched off his torch. There was no light except that at Hafod : not the light itself but a reflected glow in the thin mist. He continued, splashing up the track with the rain coming down like small projectiles on his head.

It must have been steamy indoors for Hafod's windows were open to the night. The record player was going quite loudly with what sounded like opera choruses: too gay for his mood. On an impulse he closed the gate quietly and walked forward in his rubber soles until he could see into the kitchen from the edge of the terrace. The sound of water sluicing from a blocked gutter and the rush of the swelling river, these and the music drowned other sounds.

Mollie was standing in the kitchen, doing something at the table, her eyes intent. Simon was pouring wine in a glass and lifting it to the light. He tasted it thoughtfully then offered it to her. She rolled the liquid over her tongue and for a moment which Parry envied them, they regarded each other with an intimacy the more poignant in view of its context: a verdict on wine.

He opened the door and walked in the kitchen. They greeted him quickly and, his perceptions brought to a fine point by the whisky, he saw that they were selfconscious.

Molly shoved a plate of canapés towards him; Simon poured a glass of wine and offered it. 'We think it's all right,' he said with too much emphasis. 'What do you think?'

Parry drank obediently. 'It seems a bit thin. It's difficult to tell; I've been drinking Scotch.'

Mollie frowned. 'I hope you don't have to go out tonight.'

Parry was climbing out of his waterproofs. 'What's rain?' he asked, but she hadn't been referring to the weather, and he knew it.

'Go in the other room,' Simon ordered. 'You'll find some whisky. Catrin's there.'

She was in velvet: red, he saw, when she moved and the light caught the folds. She was reading a record sleeve and as she turned on his entrance the firelight flickered on copper earrings. She looked like a hostess in a film. He accepted a whisky and asked if she'd had a good day. She said she'd been on the sea cliffs.

'How did Keith go?' he asked carelessly.

'He was a bit rattled by the exposure but he soon got used to it. It's the sea worries them the first time: they don't like the movement when they look down. There was a swell running and he found that disconcerting too.'

'I used to find it exciting.'

'What have you done here?' Ostensibly she was polite—and she'd turned down the volume on the record player.

'The only sea cliffs I'm familiar with are in Cornwall.' He hesitated. 'The stuff up here is
148

too hard for me. Except on very rare occasions I've always been at the sharp end until yesterday. It would be demoralising to be dragged up routes which were too hard for me to lead, so I don't know the Welsh sea cliffs.'

'You prefer to lead?'

'There's no risk to being second.'

Her eyebrows went up but she didn't comment. The others came in with the food and wine. Parry started to eat canapés. No one asked where Beryl was. He regarded Catrin speculatively and thought she looked tired.

Simon was watching him, the pouches under his eyes accentuated in the dim light. No one looked fresh. There was a stiffness in the atmosphere when they weren't talking: pauses filled by the background music but not adequately. Mollie cosseted him like a hostess, pushing plates of food at him, and Catrin moved about filling their glasses.

A record ended and the silence became embarrassing. Simon stretched his legs. 'They're so febrile: all these operas and comic operas,' he complained. 'Lord! Listen to that river!' Looking at no one in particular he added: 'There'll be no climbing tomorrow.'

'Oh, I don't know.' Catrin halted before Parry, holding the whisky bottle. 'It's too heavy to last, isn't it?'

'It'll probably be a glorious day tomorrow,' he agreed evenly.

She smiled. 'How about the sea cliffs?' He

closed his eyes, and opened them to see that they were all watching him.

'You want to kill me?'

Her lips parted. 'You'll love it when you get there; we'll do something easy, I promise you.'

'I've heard that before.'

'I mean it.'

The others were listening but pretending that they weren't.

'Three on the rope?' he asked doubtfully.

'Just you and me; Keith will be at work.'

He looked at her steadily and, to keep the satisfaction hidden, thought of those cliffs with the spray bursting like shellfire on the bottom pitches. 'You want to see me make a fool of myself,' he grumbled.

'We won't do anything you don't want to do. What do you think I'm trying to prove? I want a climbing partner and you're a good second. You're no good to me if you're tense.'

He was 'a good second'—and that was the kind of remark guys made of girls. He grinned emptily. 'That's better than nothing; the most I'll get from you, I suppose.'

'Count your blessings. Keith would die sooner than let his leader fall but he's not experienced, is he?' She sparkled at him. 'He'd die *and* let his leader go; what good is that to me?'

'I wonder how many of my team could hold a falling leader? Have you given any more thought to taking Gareth out?'

'Oh yes; I wasn't joking.'

'Your help is greatly appreciated,' he said stiffly, and looked at Simon to see if the big man would add anything. Simon said: 'She's got nothing else to do, and the devil finds work . . . You know the rest.'

Catrin considered this seriously. 'I might make trouble, but not to enjoy it.' She turned to Parry. 'I'm a bit careless, that's all.'

'I've noticed that.'

Mollie went to the record player and chose the Pastoral symphony. Simon nodded approval and they started to converse in a murmur. The pairing was deliberate and obvious but Parry didn't care about that. Catrin had not only humoured him but reassured him. Engaging herself to climb with him tomorrow would leave Keith at a loose end and force him back to the garage. While Parry climbed above the sea, Keith would be safe in the repair shop. The rescuer's eyes creased with pain. 'You're working through the team,' he said brutally.

The sudden attack didn't surprise her. 'Only three,' she reminded him. 'Three with Gareth. I doubt if any of the others would be worth the effort.'

'How would you know?'

'No one's recommended them.' She returned his gaze equably with that upwards slant of the mouth, the lift of her brows which implied amusement at the hint that she was sleeping her way through his men rather than teaching them how to climb. 'Do you mind?' she asked curiously.

'The pleasure's all ours.' He was ironical but he knew he couldn't embarrass her in this context. He was wondering what he should do now; he'd broken up the relationship between Keith and her but he didn't feel secure.

'What do you want?' She was watching him.

'Nothing.'

There was a pause while she considered whether the reply related to short term projects or to his life. 'You mean: you've got everything you want?'

'I didn't say that. I said I didn't want anything.'

'What's the difference?'

'If you can't see any, there's no point in trying to explain.' He was aggressive.

'I've turned a knife,' she said. 'I'm sorry; that's what I meant about being careless.'

'I hurt myself.' He feigned contrition. 'I would *like* to want things: I'd give anything to have a goal to work for, to achieve, and then go on to the next, and so on: from one to the other, like stepping stones, but I don't think anything's worth fighting for any longer.' He thought about it for a moment. 'The fun's gone.'

'You did have fun?'

'If by fun you mean being absorbed in a situation—or a climb: just thinking about that and nothing else, or, if you thought about something else, then thinking you'd rather be doing that—yes, I had fun. The trouble is, now I've got no interest in what I'm doing, but I don't want to do anything else either.'

'Like being here?'

He looked round the room carefully. 'I'm just being polite.'

'You're bored.'

'Not bored: sick.'

'What's the disease?'

'Glamour.'

'Go on.'

'You should know what I'm talking about; you were the one who stripped the last veil away.' His eyes teased her but his smile was crooked. 'I'm beginning to understand a lot of things I didn't till recently. I know what a catalyst is, for instance: something that changes substances without being changed itself, is that right? Or it could be a person. I was happy till you came—or at least I wasn't aware that I was unhappy—but that's the wrong word: unhappiness. I'm fed to the teeth.'

'With what? Who's upset you like this?'

'I don't know where it started; coming down from the hill last Sunday perhaps: the fanfares, and the jostling to take up position, and Ellis-Jones so concerned about me saying something new and not repeating myself, and all the mechanics . . . the right background for

153

the camera, the pitch of my voice. Everyone was playing a part; even the observers, like yourself, were participants: an audience for the show. The only superfluous objects were the people we brought down—and once they'd been taken away they weren't even part of the scenery.'

She nodded. 'The rescuers were the focal point. So what? They were important.'

'And next day the legend had swelled a bit more—and by that time I'd got drunk and I'd talked to you, and I'd gone home . . . It didn't hurt much to have you witness my disgrace on Monday; I'd woken up by then.' He grinned and nodded. 'That wasn't me nearly came off Hornet; that was a legend caught out. It ought to be lying at the foot of Craig y Bera now and that would have been the proper end to the legend, see? You stopped something in the middle: produced an abortion. Without you I could have gone on kidding myself; without you I'd have convinced myself I was exhausted after a weekend's rescue, and dodged the last pitch of Hornet and walked down satisfied because I'd solo-ed the rest of it. And I'd have gone to the Commercial with the lads that night where everyone would have bought me drinks because I was the Minera leader and Minera was a bunch of golden boys last Monday morning.'

'You're an ungrateful bastard,' Mollie told him and he knew they'd heard it all.

'He can't accept his pedestal,' Simon explained. 'He wants out—or off. It's no good, Owen, you've condoned what the media did and now you've got to live with what they've made of you. Fame's like rank, it carries responsibilities. *Noblesse oblige.*'

'Do you think that?' Parry addressed Catrin.

'It's one way of looking at it,' she said carelessly. 'It doesn't worry me: I don't mean fame, I mean the question of it. I can see that you find it important—' She broke off in the face of his intent stare. For a moment she studied him, then went on, at first reluctantly: 'I guess that fame and adulation must be great fun at first but like everything else that depends on performances, the applause you get will fluctuate according to whether you're performing well.' He was frowning but she continued, now interested despite herself: 'And since your base-line has to be the most sensational rescue in the past—and there can't be many of those—most of the time you'll be frustrated. Then you'll suddenly have an important rescue handed you on a plate, and you realise a high standard is demanded of you—but perhaps your standard's gone down?' Her eyes questioned him: 'Or you don't think it's worth making the effort? The performance becomes mechanical: action divorced from humanity. You find the audience contemptible.'

'You're a cool bitch,' Simon remarked.

Mollie said suddenly to Parry: 'Your book:

155

you're having difficulty with it?' He nodded. 'You've led a hell of a life,' she went on. 'I can't bear to see all your adventures wasted. How about handing the manuscript over to me and letting me write it as a biography? I can tell the truth. You can't. You're all tied up in knots at this moment.'

'What will that do for me?'

She shook her head at him dolefully. 'So egocentric you should be an author,' she observed. 'Look, I'm not concerned about you, you stupid oaf; I want your *story*. Not you, but your achievements. There are people outside Minera who need heroes. Of course, they don't know it, but there you are . . . What the hell do you think I've been trying to do for twelve years? Why do you think I did it? I wasn't blowing trumpets for a tinpot village rescue team because of the fat retainer they pay me. This is my job. You perform, as Catrin says, and I broadcast the performance. But you've been trying to be two kinds of professional: rescuer and writer. What I'm suggesting now is that you do the one and I'll do the other and we'll go back to working as a team, each to his own speciality. That way we might get the lines uncrossed. What do you say?'

CHAPTER TEN

'Do you think I was right to give Mollie my book to finish?'

'She won't *finish* it; she'll start again, using your rescues but her own interpretations.'

'Not of facts!'

'Motives, probably.' Catrin's voice was somnolent and Parry couldn't see her face.

They were sitting in pale sunshine on a rock platform above the sea. The swell had died and the water was so quiet that they could hear a cormorant beating over the surface a hundred feet below them.

'If she can see what my motives are,' he said equably, 'she's a better man than I am.'

'That's what I thought—but she'll make a good books of it.'

They lapsed into a companionable silence. He felt like an animal with winter approaching, drinking in the last of the soft warmth which had none of the passionate heat of summer about it. There was even behind the sunshine, a hint of frost borne on the breeze that nosed in shadowed corners and then wandered along the top of the cliffs where bramblings sang and chough patrolled in noisy amity.

He was enjoying himself. He hadn't expected to do so; had envisaged fear,

157

humiliation, contempt. He had been surly on the drive down here and silent as they descended to the shore. Originally she'd asked him to choose the climb and, not looking at her, he'd suggested something hard. She read the description in the guide book then, without comment, turned to others and picked unerringly the great classic on this cliff. It was easy in comparison with his own wild suggestion.

She had climbed it with predictable competence and, watching her on the first pitch, he'd been aware of the sun through the thick wool of his shirt and felt the dankness that is the ambiance of wet rock; he'd heard the wash of the waves and the bark of a seal from the depths of the cave round the corner, but he'd felt no emotion, only content.

When it came to his turn to climb, he liked it. Today nothing was extreme. The angle of the buttress was steep but not overpowering; there were no impending overhangs. The holds were small but set where they were needed; a slab could be climbed neatly, and this neatness: the holds being placed in exactly the right sequence, constituted an ordered pleasure in the correctness of things, even if that order lay only in the structure of the rock.

The handholds were good: in-cut so that the fingers curled over them like a claw on a branch—and when the slab steepened to a wall, the holds increased in size: both for hands and feet, so that where you needed the power factor more than balance, there was a launching pad.

At the top he'd asked her about his book. Now she told him to choose the next climb. They were polite and pleasant to each other. She was sitting with her legs drawn up and her chin on her knees, looking down the length of the bay to Saint David's Head at the end of the long coast of Pembrokeshire.

'Could the quality of the light originate in the expanse of sea?' she mused. 'You never get it inland.' She turned to him. 'Might you have the same kind of light in the desert: with great stretches of sand, or rock without vegetation?' He shrugged, thinking about rock, not light. 'There *is* a certain light in the desert,' she went on.

'Have you been there?'

'No. I'm going.' She spoke absently.

'When?'

'Next week.' He said nothing. 'I've got the vehicle at last and I'm cutting short my stay here. I didn't think I'd get a truck so quickly.'

'Where are you going?'

'Oh, don't you know?' She was suddenly gay and childlike. 'I thought everyone knew. I'm going to drive to Australia—discounting the sea bit, of course.'

A nerve was twitching in his cheek. 'What kind of truck?'

'It's a Land Rover. Thirty thousand on the

clock but with a new engine and a good overhaul we'll make it as good as new.'

'Clapped out,' he said distantly. 'Who's "we"?'

She looked away. 'The guy who drives my father.'

'Your chauffeur, you mean?' His tone was bullying. 'He'll need to go with you to Australia, because you're going to need a mechanic unless you're any good at that kind of thing yourself.'

'No; I'm taking a fitter—or rather, a chap with a fitter's experience.'

He pressed his fingers on the jumping nerve. He was cold and realised that the sun was sinking fast. Their cliff cast a shadow far out on the surface of the water and in the gloom the seals drifted like dark ghosts.

'Did you have anyone in mind?' She shook her head. 'I'm quite good with engines myself,' he said.

They looked at each other, Catrin amused, Parry apparently cool, almost indulgent, but his thoughts whirling so furiously that he was forced to look away to prevent her seeing them in his eyes.

*   *   *

They arrived in Cwm Daron after dark. She suggested he come up to Hafod after he'd eaten—and to bring Beryl. He had no

160

intention of doing so but he said he might, anticipating his absence by arranging to climb with her the next day.

Beryl was home, knitting by the light of the gooseneck lamp. He paused, staring through the kitchen window; that lamp should be upstairs in the bedroom where he did his work. Then he remembered that Beryl knew about the book; she'd held it in her lap when he'd driven her to work this morning, before he left it at Mollie's. Bringing the lamp down marked a change of scene.

Parry felt as if he had abandoned a part of himself. Something that had been alive even when he wasn't actively concerned with it, was now dead.

Beryl looked surprised when he asked if Gareth had called.

'Not while I've been home. Did you expect him to?'

'We've got the weekend to settle.' He moved to the telephone and dialled. 'Yes,' he said in answer to her question, 'we had a very pleasant day . . . Gareth? What do you think about the weekend? . . . I thought a rock climbing exercise; it's what they all need . . . Leaders? You've got half a dozen at least: yourself and Keith, Idris Evans . . . No—' his tone was firm, '—you can have the field to yourself this weekend; remember what we were saying: if anything happened to me, you'd be the one to take over, so it's time you got some practice in . . . Well, that's all right; if you haven't got enough leaders, divide the team: let half do a navigation exercise, and you climb with just as many parties as you've got leaders for . . . . Yes, of course you must have a deputy: that will be Keith . . . It's nothing to do with them; if I say he's to be deputy, he is. Tell him I said so . . . I'm having a few days off . . . Why should I do that? If I was in bed with a broken leg you wouldn't be able to get hold of me, would you? . . . You could use my advice?' He was smiling genially. 'All right—' he held up a hand as if Gareth were in the room with him, and winked at Beryl. 'On Saturday I'll be on the Rhinogs, so I hope you don't have any emergencies because I couldn't get there in time. You're on your own, man!'

He replaced the receiver and grinned expansively at Beryl. 'Any Scotch left?' he asked, going to the dresser himself. As he poured a drink he said with elaborate carelessness: 'I decided he should be in charge this weekend. Not before time, is it?'

'Is he good enough to be in charge of a climbing exercise? He seemed to have reservations.'

'He'll only have three or four parties on the rock and he'll see that they all stay on easy routes.'

'Are there enough leaders?'

'Gareth's all right; he's just lacking in self-confidence. He'll only take the same number

162

of novices as he's got leaders for.' She didn't comment on that but took up her knitting. Parry lit a cigarette. 'He'll have Keith to back him up.'

'Keith's going to be annoyed at having to do easy climbs when he'd been hoping to climb with Catrin this weekend.'

Who'd told her that? He breathed deeply but all he said was: 'Did you see him at work today?'

'I didn't see him on the pumps when I came home, but there were no cars waiting for petrol. He could have been in the repair shop; that's his favourite place. He wants to be a fitter . . . you knew that?'

'Yeah,' Parry said evenly, 'I knew.'

*   *   *

On the Friday morning they returned to the sea cliffs, Parry on edge now: wondering how Keith would view the weekend's arrangements, whether Gareth would have the confidence to go on with the exercise or would cancel it at the last moment. The routes above the sea seemed to conspire against him for they'd done the best climbs yesterday and now those which were left were too easy, or else too hard and with suspect rock. They didn't comment on the routes but worked their way through them stolidly.

The air was sparkling: visibility had

163

improved even since yesterday but the colour faded gradually from the sky as the day progressed. At five o'clock Catrin remarked that the wind was backing. Diagonally across the bay the mountains called the Rhinogs were humped like elephants, their gullies as prominent as if they were five miles away, not twenty.

'You see that cliff?' He pointed. 'No, of course you can't; I can see only its top and I know where to look for it. On the far Rhinog: it's got two or three good routes on it. I was thinking about it for tomorrow.'

'It's Saturday tomorrow; what about the team?'

'Gareth's in charge.'

'I thought you always went out with them.'

It was pointless to deny it because she'd have been told the truth by Simon. 'We've agreed that it would be better for Gareth to take over. You were there when we discussed delegation: you suggested it.'

'I see. And I'm leaving next week.'

'Well, you didn't want to spend your last weekend training a bunch of novices, did you?' He was jolly and out of character. She looked at him curiously.

'You've stopped me climbing with them.' It was a fact, not a protest.

'Not at all. I enjoy climbing with you; I haven't had such a good time for years. To tell you the truth: I'm exploiting you.' He looked across the water to the mountains. 'I doubt I'm too old now ever to find another chap to take me up these routes, I mean the harder ones, like The Cat, and what I was hoping for tomorrow. You've made a new man of me. No, I haven't stopped you climbing with them, but I'm certainly trying to keep you to myself.' His face dropped and he looked sullen. 'Would you have preferred to climb with them?'

'With the team? Good God, no! I'd find it wildly embarrassing.'

'Well, then?'

'I had promised Gareth—but Sunday perhaps? I wondered why you were suddenly so enamoured of my company. After all,' she added shrewdly, 'it isn't as if we were having a passionate love affair.'

He smiled weakly. 'It's killing several birds with one stone. In you I've found a good leader to take me out, and that's provided the incentive to leave the team on their own for a weekend: to give Gareth a chance to show what he's made of. It also gives the lads an idea of another guy's working methods. You can get in a rut.'

'I see. What will Keith be doing?'

'He'll back up Gareth.'

She nodded and looked at her watch. 'Is Beryl expecting you back?'

'What did you have in mind?'

'Dinner at the Lobster Pot.' He glanced at his breeches. 'Oh, never mind about clothes,' she chided. 'They're not fussy. I know them; they used to have a restaurant in Kensington.'

The only time that Parry ate in hotels was on the occasions of Rescue and club dinners which were held in places of which the only asset was that they could seat a lot of people. The Lobster Pot was small, select and very expensive.

'It's my party,' she said, watching him.

'Where do you get this kind of money?' he asked curiously. 'You're going to Australia, buying a Land Rover; you can eat at places like the Lobster Pot—?'

'I hoped I wouldn't have to confess. You know those cartoons in the commercials on the box? I do that kind of thing—did, rather. I got away.'

'Simon was in advertising too.'

'Nepotism—the old boy network. We were good though; it's just that it wasn't our scene.'

'What are you going to do now?'

'Drive to Australia.'

'I mean: when you get there.'

'I don't know.' She was surprised. 'How would I know? Does it matter?'

'Well,' he muttered, getting up with exaggerated stiffness, 'I suppose I'd have said the same thing at your age.'

*   *   *

Over dinner, which was slow and rich and

accompanied by two kinds of wine followed by brandy, he persuaded her to go to the Rhinogs next day. She didn't really need persuading and he felt that even if it were raining in Cwm Daron in the morning, she would accompany him. Hard men didn't mind a spot of rain.

The only snag was that Gareth might run into some unexpected hitch which would necessitate Parry having to postpone his own arrangements. The leader arrived home at eleven-thirty, dreading that there would be a note on the kitchen table telling him that Gareth was waiting for a call. There wasn't, and Beryl had gone to bed. He'd telephoned her from the Lobster Pot saying that he was in a pub on the coast—which was only a step away from the truth.

At breakfast the following morning she appeared to find it quite acceptable that he should be going out yet again with Catrin. He told her that the girl was leaving Wales the following week and he was having as many good climbs with her as possible before she left. It sounded lame but she accepted it and he found himself wondering if she suspected how difficult it was for a middle-aged man to find people to take him up hard routes.

Catrin arrived late but they managed to get away from the combe without running into the team, if indeed Gareth was bringing them this way. Because of the lack of communication he didn't even know where they would be this weekend. He left the Land Rover at Dolwen in case it should be needed by the team and Catrin drove them to the Rhinogs in Simon's car.

The weather was not good. It wasn't raining and the cloud was clear of the tops but the peaks stood up hard and high against a flat sky. The air was sticky and the wind was not consistent, although from the feel of the day, it would soon settle and blow hard from the south-west. When they reached the road-end on the seaward side of the Rhinogs, they packed their waterproofs in their sacks.

The cloud was lowering as they walked up the combe to the cliff and by the time they were close enough to the face that he could show her where the climbs went, the ceiling was below three thousand feet.

'How long have we got?' she asked dubiously.

'Before what?'

'Before the bad weather.'

'You don't like climbing in the wet?'

She regarded him steadily. 'There's something nasty coming up; not just rain: a lot of wind too. How long do you think before it starts to blow? I don't mind the rain.'

'Four hours perhaps.'

'I suppose I can get up this in a couple of hours,' she muttered. It was a grumble: a sign of nerves. He squinted at the sky; she was right, there was a spell of really bad weather coming. He looked northwards, across the bay. The sea cliffs were plainly visible, but the long spurs of the Rhinogs hid the Cwm Daron mountains.

'Did Simon say where the team was going?'

'No; how would he know? He's not going out with them. Are you worried?' She grinned. 'You've got to learn to delegate; after all, rescue's a matter of bad weather and darkness and being unroped.'

He winced: He tried to hold down the fear which rose like nausea, but she must have seen something of it in his face. 'Shall we go back?'

He took a grip on himself. 'No. Like you said: they've got to learn to live without me. They're big boys now.' He turned and looked up the line of the climb, but his body felt like lead.

*   *   *

It started to rain when they were fifty feet from the top. The wind had been rising all the time and she had climbed fast. He watched her stonily, listening to the sounds of falling water and measuring the duration of the gusts which so far were only strong enough to be evaluated by the way they carried sound. The cloud dropped steadily until they climbed into it, and then the temperature fell as well.

The rain came so quickly that it must have been advancing in a front across the bay. They

169

would have seen it coming if they hadn't been in the cloud. Then there was a stinging shower of hail which held them up because Catrin had to clear the holds before she could use them. She was climbing slowly now, and carefully: one of those whose standard went up in adverse conditions. He had no worries with her in the lead and when she reached the top and started to take in the rope, he felt that this was an anti-climax; it was an ordinary day after all. He was afraid that she might have been disappointed in the climb.

'Oh no,' she assured him, laughing when he apologised. 'I didn't want anything harder today—nor longer. We snatched it only just in time.'

They were now wearing their waterproofs and the rain was nothing more than a part of the view, but it was unseasonably cold. He thought it must be snowing on the tops. By the time they reached the car the wind was sweeping across the bare uplands from the sea, stripping the straggling thorn trees of leaves that were not yet dead.

They stopped in Harlech for a meal and then drove north towards what would be, on a good day, a magnificent panorama of mountains beyond woods and water meadows but now it was screened by successive waves of rain.

It was after six when they turned off the main road and visibility was so poor that

Catrin had come up the valley on dipped headlights. The entrance to the combe was murky under the cloud.

She stopped outside Dolwen and he stirred himself. Unaccustomed to someone else driving he had been lulled by the warmth and the mesmeric sweep of the windscreen wipers.

'You'll come in for a cup of tea?' he asked, but she was staring over his shoulder. He turned and saw Beryl coming across the sodden turf with a raincoat over her head. He wound down the window.

'Call-out, is it?'

'I don't know.' She acknowledged Catrin with a worried nod. 'You've just missed the others: they've gone up to Craig y Castell. They want you to follow.'

'Who's missing?'

'Keith . . .' She went on, stopped, then Catrin was speaking. Their voices were sound without meaning. He wondered how Catrin had the temerity to grip, and then to shake his thigh in Beryl's presence. He pushed her hand away and looked from one to the other, puzzled. They seemed to be communicating without reference to him. He shook his head. 'What's going on?'

'You've got all you need?' Catrin asked him.

'There's a flask indoors,' Beryl said urgently and turned back to the house.

He felt overwhelmed by helplessness without being able to identify the cause. 'What

171

can we do?' he shouted after Beryl but she
didn't hear. He turned to Catrin. 'She doesn't
care. She never did.'

'We'll go and find him,' Catrin said
pleasantly and he stared at her.

'How dark your eyes are,' he said, smiling,
but vaguely disturbed because she looked so
sad, which wasn't like Catrin.

CHAPTER ELEVEN

Rain was coming in at the open window.
Catrin made some remark and after a while he
asked her to repeat it.

'I'd like a cigarette,' she said evenly.

'Yes. Where did I put them?'

'In your anorak pocket.'

'I'm sorry.'

He brought out the packet and offered it to
her. 'I didn't know you smoked,' he said with
interest.

She exhaled slowly. 'You must ask Beryl
what happened.'

'Yes.' He looked towards the cottage as if
wondering how this might be accomplished.

'We'll go indoors.' She swung out of the car,
taking the ignition key. That annoyed him
because he felt a compulsion to be at the road-
end and he would have driven there himself if
she hadn't taken the key.

172

He got out slowly and followed her. Everything seemed to have lost substance: rain, ground, the wet wood of the gate. He touched but was unaware of contact.

When he entered the kitchen Beryl was talking as she filled a vacuum flask. The table was cluttered with dirty mugs as if she'd had a lot of visitors.

'. . . don't know much—' she was saying, hesitating as Parry appeared, then continuing: '—they were all meant to meet at Simon's but Keith and Deri didn't come down. They waited till about six and now Simon and Gareth have gone up with the team to try to see them.'

'See them?' Parry asked. 'The cloud's right down. Where are they?'

Beryl screwed the top on the flask. 'They were on Craig y Castell.'

'On—? *Today?* Which route were they doing?'

'I don't know.'

'Who saw them last?'

'I think it was Gareth, but that was at the bottom of the cliff: before they started climbing.'

'Gareth!' Parry exclaimed, and they looked at him: Beryl uneasy, Catrin speculative. 'Why did he take them on that cliff?'

'There's not much daylight left,' Catrin put in. 'We ought to get a move on—and the others are expecting you to catch them up; someone has to organise things.'

She took the flask and they went out to the car. She drove up the track, not stopping at Hafod but going on to the road-end where several vehicles were parked, all of which belonged to members of the team. They included Parry's Land Rover and Gareth's Cortina.

He went so fast up the path that Catrin dropped behind. He wasn't surprised at this; women couldn't keep up, he thought, unaware that he was functioning only on one level of consciousness. Some physical sensations were getting through to him now but only superficial ones like rain penetrating to his neck by way of a crease in his cagoule, and the wind which pounced on him as he came over the lip of the headwall, hurling him first one way then the other. Impact against a boulder was registered, but not experienced as pain, and when he felt his ankle twist in a hole or heard knuckles crack on stone he was not aware of it at the time but afterwards, as a memory.

Above the headwall he was in the cloud and the claustrophobia of mist at night was accentuated by noise: some of it consistent, like the boulders which were being pounded and rolled down the river bed, others gusting where the wind roared and smashed in the unseen gullies of the combe—and behind was the deep note of storm: a composite of wind and water and everything else that moved on a night like this.

The stream, which was the outlet from the lake under Carnedd Iago at the back of the combe, was bridged in two places by slabs of slate set on miniature piers but tonight the water was washing over the slabs and the stream had become a torrent. He crossed it twice, wading upstream of the bridges, feeling along the slabs with his hands. The water was up to his waist and between the piers the current tried to sweep his legs under the slabs.

The path turned west and the gale, now deflected slightly by the long southern spur of Craig y Castell, thundered through the combe behind him. Without that incessant buffeting he could go faster and, as the way ran level for a short distance, he started to jog, but it was too difficult to keep on the path at speed and he resumed his fast walk.

The ground steepened under the screes and, with the lessening of noise and elemental violence, he became aware of something more personal which demanded his attention. His head hurt. That was unusual; in the normal way it would be his chest, and that pain he attributed to the lungs, which was the reason why he had stopped smoking. As for his head, he had been drinking a lot lately, and there was all that wine and brandy last night. It was some time since he'd gone fast uphill; the headaches would be due to alcohol and age. He worked it out to his satisfaction but he continued more slowly.

The wind increased with altitude. He was scrambling up a shallow gully when he ran into jumbled boulders which he turned by kicking steps diagonally up steep earth at the side of the depression. As he came out on a soft bank of vegetation, he was pushed backwards by some force, gently it seemed, missed his footing, and felt the ground move as if it were water, or snow in an avalanche. Movement stopped with a painless but stupefying crash and this time, finding himself on his back, he thought he would lie there for a moment before making the effort to regain his feet. He had reached the others anyway. He could see a torch.

The light approached slowly, but probably not so slow as he imagined. A delicious feeling of relaxation permeated him; he remembered that he'd waded the stream twice but his feet weren't cold. Wriggling his toes he found that they were very wet. He should remove his boots and get rid of the water but that would mean going to all the bother of untying and unzipping his gaiters. He smiled at himself, the irritation amusing in its pettiness.

'You look comfortable there.' Catrin's voice came from behind the light. 'Did the wind catch you?'

'I suppose so. You were quick.'

'Not really. I've been behind you all the time. The river was a bit full, wasn't it?' He didn't respond. 'Can you move your legs?' she asked. He couldn't see her face, only the light.

'Of course I can.' He was petulant. 'I've only just landed. I was about to get up.' He did so but staggered against her, his hands sliding on her wet cagoule in the effort to retain his balance. She gasped and swore.

'Well,' he snapped, turning his light on her: 'Have you heard the others?'

'No.'

He gestured uphill. 'Then we'll search along the bottom till we find them.'

*   *   *

At the head of the gully they turned and, on their left, clean walls showed on the fringe of the light, walls which appeared to move as the water streamed down them. Above, the gale drove over rock and swirled in the unseen amphitheatres and this, coupled with the ease of gradient, served to bring Parry to his senses. He stopped and listened: not for voices but to the wind. At this point he knew why he was there.

'Perhaps he just got stuck,' he said in his normal voice.

'What was that?' she shouted.

'I hope they've found a cave.'

She lifted her head. 'God! I hope he's not injured—either of them. Listen! Someone's shouting!'

But it was only the team. The texture of the

cloud showed against moving lights, there were more voices, boots trampled scree and people approached raggedly, metal and wet cagoules gleaming in the mist. Suddenly, the night was populated and the wind, the rain and the rocks retreated to become a background to the men.

It was Gareth who put a stop to the confusion almost before it could begin: announcing loudly and firmly that they were on their way to have a break at the Shelter Stone. He moved down the slope, the others followed, and Catrin and Parry went with them.

The Shelter Stone was a boulder so huge that a dozen men could sit in dry comfort underneath it. Tonight there were seventeen. As rucksacks were unpacked and hot liquid started to steam, Parry looked round for Gareth but in that confined space of light and shifting shadows, he could identify no one until he heard the First Aider's voice and realised that the man was next to him.

Gareth told the story as if it were a briefing which concerned two strangers. Parry listened for one word, one note which might imply that the other saw this incident as anything different from the dozens which occurred every year, but the man seemed as unmoved as if he were talking of two hikers missing from a youth hostel.

The team exercise had been in two parts. Not many men had turned out today, and only four of those were good rock climbers. There were three leaders: himself, Keith, and Idris Evans—who was with them now. Deri George could climb but not lead. Gareth had brought four of his youth club members along: two to join the climbing party, the other pair to get some navigational practice with the rest of the team.

The three climbing parties had started on easy routes on Craig y Castell at about eleven-thirty. At that time the cloud was already below the foot of the face. The arrangement was that the climbers and the navigators should all meet back at Hafod.

Comments jostled in Parry's mind but his reactions were slow, and the compulsion to hear what had happened was greater than the urge to interrupt.

Gareth and his second had reached the summit at three-thirty and didn't linger there because a blizzard was blowing. They'd started down as soon as they'd coiled the rope, and after they'd lost about five hundred feet, they'd come on Idris and his lad eating sandwiches in the shelter of a rock. They'd continued together, reaching Hafod at four-fifteen. No one had seen Keith and Deri since eleven-thirty at the foot of the face.

Gareth stopped talking. Parry asked coldly: 'Which climb were they on?'

'Marble Buttress.'

It was certainly an easy route, well within

179

Keith's limits in the normal way—but accidents were caused by deviations from the norm: a loose hold, a falling stone . . .

'We've been up the gullies on either side for a short distance,' Gareth told him.

'The cliff's eight hundred feet high,' Parry said bleakly. 'What did you—where did you think they were while you were coming down?' He had been about to ask: 'What did you think about . . .?' He wanted Gareth to condemn himself publicly.

'I thought they were in front of us. Keith and Deri were the strongest party so I'd expected them to reach the top first and never expected them to wait—in that weather.'

'Filthy weather,' Parry conceded. No one said anything. 'So what's the plan now?' His teeth flashed as he turned on Gareth.

'You'll take over now,' the other said.

Parry looked at Simon. Most of them had switched off their lights but he'd left his own on: illuminating the others' faces without showing his own. Simon blinked and shielded his eyes.

'We've been along the bottom once,' the big man said. 'Right along, not concentrating only on the stretch below where they went up. It's possible that if they reached the summit quickly they might have decided to descend the face by an easy route, so we've been all the way along underneath—and we've shouted.'

'How far would your shouts carry tonight?'

Parry asked as if he were really curious. Simon lapsed into silence. Parry looked at his watch. 'Eight-forty,' he announced. 'And no sign of it quietening down. If they're unconscious they wouldn't answer anyway—' he paused and his hand went to his forehead, fumbled with the headlight, came away, '—and we can't get on the face—not to be safe ourselves . . .' His voice was uneven.

Simon said: 'If they're still alive, they've got into shelter—'

'Up *there*?' Parry interrupted incredulously.

'—in a cave or under an overhang,' Simon went on. 'They won't hurt till morning, Owen; the temperature's not that low. We can't do anything in the dark in these conditions; listen to it!'

Parry knew that the big man was right; moreover, in asserting that Keith and Deri would survive the night, he was trying to stiffen the others against the inevitable moment when they must turn their backs on the cliff. The leader was torn apart. Somewhere above him—in so small a span: eight hundred feet by less than a mile—Keith sat or lay within what would be shouting distance on a good day. Possibly he was alive and would live if they could reach him now but would die if he were out all night. How could he, Parry, turn downhill and head for home surrounded by the tight security of his team, and abandon the other for those few vital hours? But even though he was willing at this moment to put the team at risk, he couldn't see what they could do. No one could climb the face: the gusts would pluck them away like dead grass. They couldn't go on the ridge because there the wind was stronger. Even if he (and Catrin?) made some kind of suicidal rush up Marble Buttress, it would be nothing more than that; no one could *search*.

'Well?' Gareth asked from beside him. The men were packing up. Under cover of the bustle Parry said: 'We'll have to go down.'

'Sunrise about half past six,' Gareth murmured. 'We can be back here by six.'

The men emerged from the shelter of the boulder, stretching themselves, groaning at the discomfort of damp clothing on clammy flesh, easing on their sacks, staring upwards, their headlights slanting through cloud which moved with a spectral urgency across the beams.

*   *   *

There was no communication on the descent; at first it was too steep and greasy and all their concentration was needed to keep their footing on the jumbled scree, and when they encountered smoother ground, they were exposed to the terrible onslaughts of the wind which seemed to be increasing in velocity. The gusts were not consistent in direction for they swirled in the upper combe and no one knew whether the next blow would come from the right or the left, from behind or in front. Below the lip of the headwall it was comparatively quiet but the men still staggered although now it was with exhaustion.

Mollie had joined Beryl at Dolwen and the women fed the team before the men went to sleep in the barn. Simon, Catrin and Gareth stayed behind in the kitchen.

The clearance of the crowd left a tense silence in a room which appeared strangely empty. Parry looked across at Gareth and was so appalled at the enormity of what the other had done that he was speechless. Gareth caught his eye and at last Parry saw that the man was suffering. His own lips tightened in grim approval: like a hanging judge observing the first signs of remorse in a killer.

'I miscalculated,' Gareth admitted. 'I thought we could do it in the time.'

'Do what?' Catrin asked.

'Complete the climbs.'

'Hell—you did!'

'I don't know . . .'

Catrin said: 'You and Idris Evans had youth club lads with you: kids. Keith and Deri were rescuers, both of them, so theirs was the strongest party. But it was the *weakest* parties which got to the top and came down without any incidents, so you didn't miscalculate, did you?'

Gareth sighed and glanced at Parry. 'I'm afraid what's happened makes Keith and Deri the weakest party.'

Parry flushed but his brain was too tired to follow the argument. All he could say in protest was: 'They were both in the team!' But in some way he felt that this was disparaging Keith and even the team itself. He wanted to go to sleep but when he thought of the dry warm bed in the room above, he remembered Keith out in the storm, perhaps in pain, and the thought of sleep was another form of betrayal.

Catrin continued to address Gareth: 'You calculate the obvious risks when you start a climb. You must have considered the weather, the type of route, whether the leaders were competent to do it.'

'Yes.' Gareth sounded tired. 'I did that—and there were the hours of daylight—I thought of that. I thought I covered everything.'

'Not the unpredictable,' she reminded him. 'No one can do that.'

Parry found his voice. 'What do you know about it?' he asked acidly.

'As much as you about the accident,' she told him, unruffled. 'And a damn sight more about climbers.'

'Now look.' Simon raised his voice: 'This isn't going to get us anywhere. We can argue about blame afterwards although—' he looked at Parry fixedly and his tone carried a warning,

'—for my money, and if you insist on apportioning responsibility, that could rest with more than one person. But we'll leave that for now and plan for tomorrow. First light around six o'clock so we'll need to get up about four-thirty. How many climbing parties are you going to put on the cliff, and where do the non-climbers go? How many other teams do we put on stand-by tonight?'

'We don't need anyone else,' Parry protested. 'Let's keep it in our own team, for God's sake!'

Surprise and a certain wariness greeted this outburst but it was Simon who said calmly: 'We'd stand a better chance of finding them if we had another team, Owen.' His glance travelled round the room, resting for a moment on Catrin. 'We've got enough climbers to search the vicinity of Marble Buttress, but not enough to rescue two injured men from a big cliff; that's when we'd need a lot of experts.'

'Suppose they descended the cliff after finishing Marble Buttress,' Catrin observed. 'We could do with putting parties on the traditional ways of descent.' She looked at Parry thoughtfully. 'Although it's unlikely that Keith would try to descend that face in the wet; he wasn't much more than a novice.'

Gareth said: 'I don't think he would look on himself as a novice.' He glanced at Parry as if for confirmation and the leader was torn

185

between the need to protest that Keith was an able climber with sound judgement, and his own condemnation of Gareth's action in sending an inexperienced lad up a serious cliff in worsening weather. Even his loyalty for one person was torn two ways.

Mollie had come in from the dairy where the two older women had been washing up. 'Surely you start with certainties?' she ventured. 'Gareth said they started up this Marble Buttress so you do that first, and it's only when you don't find them there that you start looking over the whole cliff.'

They deferred to Parry. 'We'll start on the buttress,' he agreed, and turned to Catrin. 'If we can get on it in the gale.'

She shrugged. 'It could moderate by morning. In any case, we can go up the gullies; the chances are, if they'd come off, they'd be in the gullies anyway; when people fall from a buttress, they go off the side, they don't fall down the line of it.'

'I can't see Keith coming off that climb,' Parry murmured.

'Perhaps Deri came off; perhaps he was leading and he pulled Keith . . .'

'We're wasting energy,' Simon interrupted. 'We don't even know that they're on the cliff.'

'What!' Parry was astonished. 'Where else could they be? You're not suggesting they could have reached the top and then gone wrong: walking down? You're mad.'

'It's an idea,' Catrin said coolly. 'How good were they on navigation?'

'You have to be joking.' Parry's tone was flat. She didn't repeat the question and it hung between them, unanswered.

'There's another possibility,' Gareth said. 'They might have got to the top sooner than anyone else: have climbed very fast, in fact, and then decided not to come straight down to Hafod but to do something else. Suppose they reached the top about two o'clock: the gale wasn't all that bad then.'

'What would they have done?' Simon asked, then answered his own question: 'They could have walked round the Skyline Route.'

'But if they did that—' Parry cried, looking at them wildly: 'If they did that, they could be anywhere; they could be on any one of a dozen cliffs!'

'It widens the search,' Gareth admitted. 'But which is more likely: that one of them fell on a very easy buttress and pulled the other off—and yet we heard nothing and there's no sign of them at the foot of the cliff, or that they attempted to walk at least part of the Skyline, were overtaken by the bad weather, decided to come off—'

'—And came down into a combe they didn't know.'

Catrin completed it for him. 'And they're sitting in a cave at this moment waiting for dawn?'

187

'Or one of them's broken a leg,' Gareth said.

Simon looked at Parry. 'We've got to have more men.'

Parry got up and moved to the telephone to call out the other teams.

CHAPTER TWELVE

Next morning it was still raining. Parry opened the barn doors and fastened them back, shouting to the men that it was four-thirty. He waited until several were awake. They groaned a lot as they regained consciousness, and not without cause. They would be stiff and bruised after last night. His own body felt as if it had been brutally tortured.

'You know where the tap is,' he reminded them. 'Look sharp; we're moving out at five.'

'Christ!' someone exclaimed. 'Listen to the river! The roads will be flooded.'

The gale died with the night and dawn was like a hundred other dawns: grey, cheerless and far too warm. The rain stopped as they toiled up the screes and he reflected that whatever disadvantages the night might possess, the darkness did hide the seemingly endless gradient, the ugliness of the path, the robot movements of his party and their stony faces. He felt irresolute; even the decision to stop and remove their waterproofs became a major one, but someone else stopped, breaking the rhythm of following boots. He turned angrily and saw Catrin peeling her cagoule over her head. He swung his pack to the ground and the rest followed suit.

'Now it'll throw it down!' No one responded. Resuming the path, he thought savagely that no uninformed observer would suspect that two lives might depend on the speed and enthusiasm of this group; they looked as much involved with the job as Council roadmen.

There were only six of them heading for Craig y Castell. Simon and the bulk of the team were making for the crest of the ridge to walk round the Skyline Route. The Minera team would approach the highest point: Carnedd Iago, from the south while three other teams were covering the approaches from the remaining quarters.

They came to a small cairn at the foot of a steepening so featureless in the gloom that only an expert could have identified their position. Parry sent Idris Evans and a powerful fellow called Thomas to the gully on the left and then he paused, looking at Catrin.

'Would you mind taking the other gully?' he asked.

'Not at all.' She was surprised that he should make a request of it rather than an order.

The buttress was harder than her gully

although both were easy climbs. The reason why he wanted to take the buttress himself was that he felt in this specialised field of picking up clues, he was superior to her. Even if Keith wasn't on the buttress there might be some indication of which way they'd gone if, say, they hadn't reached the top but traversed away to the side. He couldn't see why they should do this, but as Catrin had suggested last night: it was the unpredictable that happened.

He sent Gareth into the right-hand gully with Catrin. He'd included the First Aider in the party against his will; this morning he found that he was literally shrinking from the man if their paths crossed. But he couldn't ignore the fact that if the missing men were on the cliff, they were almost certainly in need of medical treatment—and he didn't trust himself. Besides, he had too few climbers. The second man on his own rope was called Pugh: a long-haired, clumsy lout who was little more than another pair of eyes, but it was eyes that were needed on a trip like this.

As he climbed, he heard snatches of conversation on either side, then long silences broken by calls. They used names when they remembered so that calls would not be confused between the parties. These disembodied comments which spoke of progress up the great cliff, and the odd little garnish of Christian names, lent an intimacy to the occasion which was curiously moving. At times he forgot how much he hated Gareth.

He was carrying a radio and at the first stance he tried to pick up Simon on the ridge but the terrain was unfavourable. However, he managed to get through to Base at the road-end and to relay a message to the team that the climbing parties had started up the cliff.

At the second stance he was turning outwards after belaying when he recoiled in horror, shielding his face as an enormous shape loomed up at him. Pressed against the rock, he glared in dawning comprehension: where there had been immobile mist there was now swirling movement, increasing the illusion of attack. Colour heightened the shock, but it was the cloud that moved, the colour was static.

For hour after hour: in the dark and in the daylight, on the Rhinogs as far back as yesterday, on the road, through the rain and right up until a moment ago, the world had been one of shadowed shapes, and even the most brilliant objects: waterproofs, helmets, packs, had paled to ochre and washed-out rose.

Now, like a vision in the Dolomites, sunlit lilac pinnacles were framed in a window in the cloud. Above them the sky was gentian-blue and across a restricted space that yet suggested space vaster than the extent of one man's compass, a vapour trail streamed from a silver aeroplane.

He said nothing and as the others gained altitude he heard awed exclamations when they caught their first sight of a break in the cloud.

More windows appeared, were filmed by wraiths and fingers and ghosts of mist, and cleared again. Holes were torn, filled up—and suddenly a whole mass would dissolve to reveal acres of slanted rock, wet from the interior of the clouds and plunging into the cauldron below. But wet and sinister as the face appeared, above them the crest carried a luminosity which spoke of a quiet warmth and dry friendly rock.

After a while they realised that if the mist was going to clear it would take its time. At the moment it was merely sinking a little but this, in conjunction with their steady gain in height, meant that they were leaving it behind. Slowly and reluctantly the long arms relinquished them and they emerged above a cloud-sea, the upper level of which lay below three thousand feet and out of which the mountains humped like dark monsters asleep on the surface of an alien ocean.

As the buttress, almost a flying buttress, fined down to lie against the main bulk of the face, the gullies on either side converged and, looking down from the spine of his arête, Parry saw the others below. No trace of the missing men had delayed their progress and he could see no rope or body in the upper reaches of the gullies. The rock above him was equally bare. Sluggishly his brain started to reject the theory that Keith was on this cliff and to concentrate on the mass of possibilities which meant limitless permutations—unless they had come to grief in descending the face. He started to scrutinise the walls now exposed to view and at that point Simon came through on the radio. A body had been found in a stream to the north-west of Carnedd Iago.

'Who is it?' he asked automatically, and without hope.

It had only just been spotted, he was told; it lay in a pool below a waterfall and people were climbing down to it now. Simon went off the air in order to communicate with the radio operator in the other party. Parry brought his second up correctly, even remembering to give the right calls. He made no move to communicate with the other parties although he could see them quite well.

'What's happened?' Pugh asked as he came in sight and saw his leader's face. Parry held up his hand; Simon was on the air again.

'Red cagoule and over-trousers,' the big man enunciated clearly through the static. 'Blue anorak, white helmet . . .'

'For God's sake,' Parry cried silently. 'The hair—what about the hair?'

'—*white* helmet, Owen; which one's that?'

They could have changed helmets; it wasn't foolproof . . . 'Hair,' Parry croaked: 'Long or short?'

His shock was infecting Pugh who stared at him in mounting horror.

'Short hair,' Simon was saying. 'It's Deri George . . .'

He continued talking but Parry wasn't listening. He was watching Gareth a hundred feet below as he handed slings to Catrin in the quiet intimacy of climbers meeting on a stance. Pugh followed his glance and at that moment Gareth looked up, then Catrin, the rope in her hands partly coiled. It was she who broke the silence.

'What is it?'

'They've found Deri.'

'Is he all right?'

'No.'

She moved closer to Gareth.

'He's dead,' Parry called.

For a long moment they continued to stare upwards, then she turned and spoke to the First Aider. She must have been speaking because her pose lost its rigidity, her arms moved in small soothing gestures, she shifted her footing. Gareth remained motionless. She looked up again, her face paler, even at a distance.

'What about Keith?' she called.

'Nothing yet. I'll see you at the top.'

He moved to a point from which Idris was visible, and told him. The other lifted an arm in acknowledgement and continued climbing.

Simon and the others were on the summit. They had spread a map on a flat rock and weighted it down with stones. The place where the body had been found was marked by a pencilled cross. In a straight line the site was two miles from the summit of Carnedd Iago and in the opposite direction from Cwm Daron.

'It narrows the search,' Simon said.

Parry nodded. He didn't think Keith had been drowned as well although he wasn't surprised that one of them should have been. Falling in a flooded stream wasn't an unusual occurrence; often it happened when the survivor of an initial accident was going down to the valley for help and being careless about precautions. Of course, there was a chance that Keith had collapsed, recovered, wandered in delirium and fallen in the water, but it was unlikely. Exposure victims seldom if ever recovered under their own steam, so it was like that Keith was higher on the mountain than the body, possibly a lot higher because Deri could have been carried some distance by the stream.

'Not all that high,' Simon demurred. 'Bodies don't go easily down a rocky bed; they snag. I wouldn't think he'd have gone in far above the waterfall.'

That was at something over one thousand feet. It looked as if Keith might be found between the summit of Carnedd Iago and the waterfall. They were thinking that he had broken a leg or otherwise been immobilised, and that Deri had left him to go for help.

The other teams were summoned by radio and now the search was confined to a limited area being swept by over a hundred people. It was still a big area but not nearly as extensive as the whole range.

They were helped by the weather. As the day progressed, the cloud-sea sank and finally dispersed. Visibility in the rain-washed air was perfect and since this side of the mountain was composed of rounded ridges with bowl-shaped corries where crags could be surveyed through binoculars, it assumed the qualities of a textbook operation. Everything was in their favour. Parry remembered that he had felt that way a week ago when they were about to lower the injured schoolboy down Craig y Castell. He remembered Keith's face when he was having difficulty in tying a bowline.

The stream in which the body had been found drained a shelving corrie with lakes on two levels. The upper lake was small and there was a scree slope between its shore and the foot of a craggy outcrop. The latter possessed one grassy gully and two or three broken buttresses. The whole could be studied through glasses but to make certain that Keith had not crawled into a hole in the gully, two men were sent to climb it.

So far as the smoother part of the corrie was concerned, it was being swept by the four teams, and from a knoll above the lower lake, Parry could see the lines of men working across the slopes, some straggling, others well spaced. The bad teams were never more obvious than on a sweep search. Here and there on the skyline a radio operator stalked absently: the link between Base, Parry and the teams.

On the other side of the lower lake a black and vegetated cliff dropped sheer into deep water. It had been inspected through binoculars without result but there were gullies, chimneys, caves, where a body might wedge, and it was a bad place to go. And there was the lake. Bodies floated for a while before they sank but not if they were wearing heavy packs, boots and sodden clothing. They might have to bring in divers.

He had a large-scale map in front of him on the turf. The map was marked with pencilled lines delineating the limits of each sweep. There were ten groups forming lines in the great bowl working outwards from the stream. They were not looking only for a man but for his pack or any discarded clothing. Exposure victims were liable to throw away their clothes, even to undress, and that in the most bitter weather.

Some time before noon a glove was found in the upper corrie. It was soaked by rain but it was thought that it had not been there for long. Parry said that it should be shown to the Minera team to see if anyone recognised it. He couldn't remember what kind of gloves Keith wore. It had been hot on the day they climbed The Cat.

While he was waiting to hear the result of that, a party just below the lip of the upper corrie found a rucksack. It was unmistakable this time: one of a bulk lot Parry had ordered from the maker. It was lying in the grass of a shallow depression half a mile from the big cliff above the lower lake and on the same level, so Keith wasn't in the water. In fact, Parry thought with mounting tension, focusing the glasses on the spot where the pack had been found, they must be very close to him.

They found him shortly afterwards. He was sitting under a large boulder with his legs drawn up and his hooded head on his knees. It was such a natural position that at first they thought he was asleep.

Parry arrived to find them waiting for him, withdrawn a little from the rock. He stooped and felt the cold hard neck. With his other hand he tried to lift the head but it was rigid in the posture in which Keith had died. He looked for help and his eyes were held by Catrin who looked interested and not unkind but who made no move to assist him. He drew back from the seated figure and absorbed the details, seeing that there was no mark of violence, no distorted limbs, no sign of how or why it had happened.

Someone approached deliberately and stopped. Parry was still looking in Keith's direction although he no longer saw the body. 'The stretcher's coming up,' came Gareth's voice. 'We can release some of these men to take Deri down; there's a second stretcher on its way to the waterfall.'

Parry didn't respond. He was aware of movement but not of its significance and the next voice he heard was Catrin's.

'Should you be in charge of the other party?' she asked calmly. 'Or do you want to stay here?'

When he looked at her he saw that she was distressed. He didn't realise that her eyes were reflecting something of himself. He didn't answer her. After a moment he felt a touch on his wrist and saw that she was holding out a lighted cigarette.

'That's nice,' he said and, carrying it to his lips, inhaled like an addict.

She sat down and addressed him occasionally without evoking further response, then Gareth came back and people were talking about routes of evacuation and times of arrival. Parry listened to the sound of their voices but he felt as divorced from reality as if he were partially anaesthetised. Movements were only dimly discerned like those of gowned figures about an operating table. After a while he turned to face downhill, which seemed more natural. Catrin gave him another cigarette.

A familiar bustle alerted him; he must have been dropping off to sleep. He saw the stretcher party arriving but he couldn't remember why he'd sent for it.

Catrin suggested that he should stand up and he rose obediently. She took his arm and led him away as if she wanted to say something confidential. Behind him the stretcher was moved up the slope. Voices were suddenly hushed.

'What's going on?' he asked Catrin suspiciously.

'Just putting him on the stretcher, that's all.' He spun round and she moved to intercept him. 'I thought you wouldn't want—'

'It was my job!' he cried, and pushed her out of the way.

He rushed back to the others and flung them aside violently. Keith lay on the stretcher. Someone else had straightened the body. The eyes were closed and the long damp hair clung to the neck as if it were alive. Gareth covered the face and they started to pass the straps over the stretcher.

He moved away, to be stopped by a hard hand. 'You're going on the front,' Simon said. 'You can't leave the others to bring him down.'

He went back and took his place on the front of the stretcher.

CHAPTER THIRTEEN

It was the kind of evening that comes occasionally after a bad storm: quiet and mellow, with only the white water in the streams to show what the previous night had been like. Rabbits had come out to play in the meadows and a few house martins were flickering round a barn, feeding late broods.

Standing by the barnyard gate, watching the birds, Parry knew that it was a beautiful evening but he derived no pleasure from it, rather he was overwhelmed with sadness to think that Keith would never see fine evenings again, nor the first snow on the tops, nor a cloud-sea. He had been sitting under a rock this morning when the mist fell back to the valleys leaving the uplands bare—but he hadn't seen it.

It was incredible to remember how much time had elapsed since his last sight of the lad alive; it had been on Craig y Bera after they'd climbed The Cat. Again he saw the other turn and call over his shoulder, carelessly: 'Thanks for the climb, Dad.' Parry groaned and leaned his head on the gate, clutching the old wood with both hands, wanting to crush it.

Something touched his leg.

'Heel, Bracken!' It was the colonel's voice. He'd come up the track quietly, preceded by his Labrador.

Colonel Grainger was a spry old man, tall but a little stooped, with a large nose and a moustache stained by nicotine. He regarded Parry shrewdly. 'A bad thing this; I was on my way to offer my condolences. If you're walking down, I'll walk with you.'

Parry hadn't been going anywhere; he'd come out because he found the cottage claustrophobic. It didn't matter which way he went so he started to stroll down the track with the old man. When Parry said nothing the other went on: 'Good job the weather cleared for you. That was a severe storm last night. Gusts of a hundred miles an hour recorded on the Anglesey coast, I hear.'

'It was forecast,' Parry said. 'There were gale warnings.'

The colonel was uneasy at the other's manner. What he knew about rescue had been picked up from Parry's random information over the years.

'Bad-weather training, was it?'

'I haven't been told.'

The old man stopped short and gazed at him in consternation. 'Weren't you there?'

Parry returned his stare. 'Do you think I'd have sent them out in that? Gareth Lloyd was in charge.'

'Good Lord!' The colonel moved forward. 'Where were you?'

'I took the day off. I was on the Rhinogs.'

'Poor chap.' The next words showed whom the colonel meant. 'He'll be taking it badly: conscientious fella. I knew Lloyd was on the cliff with Keith and Deri George but I assumed that you were in command of the exercise. Didn't you know where they were going?'

'No.'

'That's bad. And you're the leader.'

'Leaders have to delegate sometimes.'

'Oh, yes; that's essential in all commands. But you know that terrible Americanism: "the buck stops here"? Trite, but I've always thought it true. Lost some men meself in the War—*first* war, you know—but it came back to me as a subaltern even if the N.C.O. was at fault. Then I suppose someone above me got the rap, eh? And there's no one above you.' Parry said nothing. 'You've been lucky not to lose any men before this in ten years.'

'Twelve years. I never lost any because I was careful.'

'How can you be careful on a rescue? You've often told me you have to take risks that you'd never even consider taking in the normal way. I know how dangerous it is.'

'Keith wasn't on a rescue,' Parry said tightly.

'That's so.' The old man shook his head. 'Terrible thing to happen. We've got Blodwen at the house. Mrs Grainger insists on her staying with us tonight. You'll be coming in to see her.'

Parry's eyes were naked and horrified. 'Do I have to?'

'Ah now, it's the worst part, isn't it: either telling the relatives or meeting them the first time afterwards? Rather be under fire, meself. But it's part of the job. Parry: he was one of your men. And then you've got to consider her feelings in the matter. I'm sure she'd want you to speak to her.'

'Has Gareth spoken to her?'

The colonel stopped and, groping in his pocket, brought out a packet of Park Drive and proffered it.

'Are you holding Gareth responsible?' he asked carefully.

Parry's eyes wandered. 'What else can I do? I wasn't there.'

The colonel smoked for a while in silence, staring at the trees above the track. At last he said: 'At one time infantrymen did their training with live ammunition. Not any more; they lost too many men. But, for my money, it saved lives in the long run; by Jove, those fellas kept their heads down when it came to enemy fire. They weren't over-cautious but they'd been trained what to expect. And Commandos. Now that's another thing, and nearer your line of duty. Ever been to Cornwall?' Parry nodded. 'Went down there in the last war on a visit to a training unit,' the colonel went on. 'Saw their chaps learning to climb on the sea cliffs. It looked pretty hazardous to me but that was nothing to the approach. They traversed at sea level. You'd be looking down from your safe perch at the top to a rough sea pounding the cliffs and it would go back, leaving a reef as fine as a long fin and these chaps would come leaping along the top and jump for the cliff between the breakers—and dammit Parry, those waves came down like pile-drivers; there'd have been no chance for anyone who fell in. And d'you know what they had on their feet? *Nailed boots!*'

'They wear rubber soles now,' Parry said.

'They told me they never had a course without a broken leg, and sometimes a chap drowned—it was the undertow, d'you see. But they turned out some good men, Parry, and you don't need me to tell you that a chap who learns to cope with fear in one field can cope anywhere. Character-building's an outdated phrase nowadays but it works still.' His eyes challenged Parry to contradict him.

'What you're saying is that because my men operate in filthy conditions, they should train in bad weather. That's true, but you build them up slowly, not throw them in at the deep end.'

'I wouldn't be too sure about that.' The colonel ruminated, sucking his moustache.

205

'No, I don't agree with you there. I think—mind you, I may be wrong—but I think your job has close resemblances to training soldiers. Your enemy is fear too: of the elements, of heights, of falling. They've got to learn to conquer that fear—' Parry made a gesture of impatience, '—not to eradicate it but to recognise it and go on working although they're afraid. That way it's pushed out of the mind. You can identify chaps with that potential very quickly in the right conditions. Now, you can't waste time and energy training men who've got no potential. You could take a year to train one slowly and then find he's frightened the first time he's in the firing line—that means, in your case: out in a big storm on his own. So what do you do?' He paused and Parry eyed him with hostility. 'You introduce your chaps to foul conditions early on: weed 'em out. Survival of the fittest, eh?'

'How many would I have left?' Parry was ironical.

'Plenty of men in Minera doing nothing,' the other reminded him sombrely.

The rescuer grimaced, thinking of them. 'And you think Gareth was doing just that: baptism under fire?'

'Gareth?' The old man was uneasy. 'No; I was merely advancing a theory.'

'It doesn't apply; my men have got to master all the techniques first.'

'What techniques?'

206

Parry was furious. 'Why: of rope management, how to climb . . . Christ! There are a thousand things they've got to learn . . . Training soldiers and training rescuers are a world apart except—' his eyes glittered, '—except for discipline. You believe in discipline, don't you?'

'Oh, yes.'

'Well—' Parry was quieter. 'Keith and Deri George sloped off on their own from the top; they wouldn't have done that if I'd been there.'

'You've got to be sure you're delegating to the right man,' the colonel pointed out. 'And yet I would have said Lloyd was a good disciplinarian. He's an excellent teacher; he runs the youth club.'

'Teachers can never keep discipline on the hill.'

'Sure of that? You're saying it because you have to go out to so many school parties in trouble. Aren't you forgetting all the teachers who don't have trouble? And Lloyd is a cut above the others. He *is* a mountaineer, he's in a rescue team, takes his youth club on the hill. He's never had an accident.'

'Until now.'

The colonel sighed. 'There are always the tearaways. You know how many times young Keith came up before the Bench. He wasn't a boy amenable to discipline.'

'With me he was.'

* * *

Blodwen was in the drawing-room with the colonel's wife: an angular woman with kind eyes. Parry didn't know what to do. He wondered if he should make some gesture like shaking hands with Blodwen. She was embarrassing with her hair untidy and her mouth trembling slightly like that of an old woman when she wasn't speaking. He had to say something; he could see from Mrs Grainger's expression that it was his move.

'I'm sorry, Blodwen,' he said awkwardly in a low voice.

'That's all right,' she whispered and then, louder: 'It was good of you to come down.'

'It was the least I could do.'

Mrs Grainger nodded approval. 'Sit down, Parry.' The colonel handed him a whisky. His wife went on pleasantly: 'Blodwen was telling me about the day Keith went climbing with you and Catrin Massey on Craig y Castell, weren't you, dear?'

Parry winced. Were they going to talk about Keith when he was *alive*? It was all over. He didn't want to remember him when he was living because this accentuated his death.

Trance-like, Blodwen said: 'He did enjoy himself those few days. He told me about it, and particularly that day on the sea cliffs—'

'He was a promising lad,' Parry blurted.

'He thought the world of you, Owen. I wish

208

he'd known—'

'The team's going to miss him,' Parry put in quickly then, aware of Mrs Grainger's regard, he took the plunge: 'I was hoping he'd form one of the nucleus the best chaps that is, who do the difficult rescues. He had the makings of a great climber.'

Blodwen smiled proudly. 'Owen thought Keith would be the leader one day.'

There was a small astonished silence.

'Good as that, was he?' the colonel barked.

Parry said gently, trying to imply that Blodwen's statement had been an exaggeration but dreading that she would contradict him: 'He was only starting, but someone has to take over eventually, and I'm getting a bit long in the tooth to be out with them all the time. Keith was used to working with the men, and he was keen.'

He saw that the colonel was puzzled; he'd be trying to equate this view with Parry's condemnation of Gareth in taking the lad to a cliff that was beyond his powers in the conditions. But he hadn't died on the cliff . . . It was the storm. He couldn't think coherently. 'You don't throw them in at the deep end—' even potential leaders. Wouldn't the old fool remember that he'd said that?

'Who will take his place now?' Blodwen asked.

Parry flinched. 'I'll have to look for another bright lad; in the youth club, maybe.'

He glanced at Mrs Grainger and remembered that they'd had a son: killed in the last war. She didn't look like a mother, he thought irrelevantly.

'Miss Catrin will be upset.' Blodwen was following her own thoughts.

Mrs Grainger frowned and Parry felt the colonel watching him. 'She is,' he agreed and then quickly, before Blodwen could continue: 'She's leaving next week—this week, and driving to Australia.'

'She told us.' Mrs Grainger smiled. 'Young girls are so adventurous these days. Has she found a vehicle yet?'

'She's bought a Land Rover.'

'She asked Keith if he'd go with her,' Blodwen said. 'Of course, it was only a joke: said she needed a good mechanic on the trip. I told him she didn't mean it but he wouldn't have that; he was sure she was serious. He's a wild boy—' she shook her head in dreamy wonder and smiled, '—had to tell me all about the countries he'd go through . . . got his school atlas out . . .' Her voice trailed away and her face creased in agony.

* * *

The colonel saw him to the door. 'You see,' the old man said: 'She doesn't blame anyone.'

'The question of blame didn't come up.'

'And won't.' The other was firm. 'She thinks

all the men in the team are heroes—and you're their leader; it would be cruel to disillusion her.'

'You've taken our measure, haven't you?' The bitterness of it made the other start.

'I didn't mean that—and I know how you feel. It's been a heavy blow for you, I can see that—and I had no idea that you set so much store by young Keith. It's bad to lose anyone under your command but to lose a man you're grooming to take over from you: that's a tragedy.' The old man looked across the yard. 'It couldn't have made him more reckless, could it?' He was speaking softly, almost to himself.

'What do you mean by that?'

'Arrogant? No, not young Keith: an innocent lad, wild certainly but not bad.' He turned to the other. 'I was wondering if, knowing he was better than the others, he was inclined to push things.'

'He didn't know.'

'But his mother said—'

'He was absenting himself from work. Roberts was threatening to give him his cards. I tried to get Blodwen to force him to see that he wasn't doing himself any good. I told her what was in my mind, but not him. I didn't see him again—after I told Blodwen. I would have told him, of course.'

'A pity you didn't perhaps. Some chaps go better if you give them responsibility. Going

211

absent from the garage, was he? What was he up to? Not that it matters now. No, I don't want to know. It's all over. We've got to accept it.'

*　　*　　*

Dusk was falling as he trudged up the track. The mile to Dolwen seemed interminable and he was exhausted. At last he wanted something: to get into bed and fall asleep. Sleep, like death, was oblivion and now he had physical pain to escape from in addition to the poignant memories of the last twenty-four hours which did not recur but were present all the time in his mind to float to the surface even as other people talked. The memories were visual: the men under the Shelter Stone with tea steaming in the torch light, the break in the mist and the violet pinnacles, the tilted expanses of wet rock gleaming from the cloud—all unbearable because at those times there was still hope. But these faded before the last picture: of the hooded figure left behind by the storm like a dead bird on the tide-line.

The pain was in his head. At the end of that slow mile he had come to appreciate it, for now it was as much constriction as pain and before it the images faded.

Beryl was knitting. She would always be knitting. She'd heard his step on the flags of the path and was watching the door as he came in the kitchen. As she caught sight of his face she gave a start of concern.

'What happened? Aren't you well?'

'I'm worn out—and I've got a hell of a head.'

'I'll get some aspirins. Sit down while I fill a hot water bottle.'

The fuss was vaguely reassuring. He sat in his chair and shielded his eyes from the light.

She didn't ask him where he'd been and he didn't feel like telling her. After he'd taken the aspirin he went to bed.

He dozed and woke in such agony that he couldn't bear to move but he managed to nudge Beryl and she woke quickly. He asked her to get him some more aspirins and a drink of water.

'Do you think you ought to take more? You had three.'

'I don't care if they kill me; this head's driving me mad.'

After the second dose he did sleep, to be wakened by the mattress lifting as Beryl left the bed.

'How's your head?'

'Not so bad now. Are you making a cup of tea?'

'Of course. Would you like me to stay at home today?'

'Hell, I'm not ill!'

She brought him tea and it revived him. His

head was certainly better now. He'd thought several times lately that he could be suffering from migraine but he'd always sheered away from the thought, preferring to blame the bouts on whisky. He'd had a large one at Bryn Mawr. Was it possible to become allergic to spirits as one grew older?

Beryl left for work but he stayed in bed. He didn't feel like eating breakfast and if he went downstairs there was nothing to do—except, he reminded himself, to clear up the mess in the Land Rover and to write his report. He couldn't face that. He would ask Gareth—no, not Gareth! Simon would do it for him.

He slept again and woke to the familiar sound of the front door opening. There were steps on the stairs and his father appeared in the doorway. The old man nodded at him.

'Bit under the weather, are you?'

'I'm all right. Did Beryl tell you?'

'She called on her way to work. You ought to see the doctor about those headaches.'

Parry's mother had died of a tumour on the brain. Meshach saw something in his son's eyes and went on quickly: 'Could be you're drinking too much.'

'Could be.'

His father moved Parry's clothes to the chest of drawers and sat down in the only chair.

'How's your arthritis?' Parry asked.

'Better today. It's the wet weather seeks it

out.'

The old man studied the floor with his big hands between his knees. 'I've just left Mrs George.'

'How is she?'

'Bearing up, like Mrs Williams. I called at Bryn Mawr on my way here.'

Parry slid down the bed so that he could look at the ceiling instead of his father. 'So you got the full story.'

'No one's got that, boy, nor ever will have. I'm sorry about those two lads. His mother tells me you intended Keith for leader.'

'She's building it up in her mind. I was considering him.'

'Yes. Beryl told me you'd made him deputy leader.'

'*What!*' He jerked upright and pain shot through his skull.

'You telephoned Gareth on Thursday night,' Meshach went on steadily, 'and said Gareth was to be in charge because you were taking the day off, and Keith was to be his deputy.'

'Oh that! I'm starting a new system: delegating power. They'll take it in turns to be in charge when I'm not there.' He remembered the colonel's words. 'It will weed out the fittest.'

'You chose the wrong weekend.'

'No one has to tell me that. You're turning the screw, Dad.'

'I'm only warning you.'

'*Warning* me? About what?' But it was empty bluster; he could guess what was coming.

'People talk. It's the natural thing for them to ask where you were.'

'And where was I?'

'Oh, I know, boy. You were out with Simon Massey's sister, and for two days before that.'

'So what? She's a climber; she could have been a man for all the difference it made.'

'Not in Minera. You're a married man and you were out for three days with a girl—and all one evening.'

Parry gaped at him. 'And where was I then?'

'In the Lobster Pot.'

'Christ! Where were you? Hiding behind the curtain?'

Meshach ignored the sarcasm. 'The only thing I can say for you is that you didn't try to hide it, just the opposite. That Land Rover with the mountain rescue boards is about as inconspicuous as a gull in a flock of crows.'

'O.K. So I went out to dinner with a girl— and before you start nagging me for spending money on another woman: she paid.'

'I knew you couldn't. But how does it look for Beryl: you having three days holiday with a girl young enough to be your daughter, and your wife slaving away in the factory?'

'You make it sound as if I was living on immoral earnings. Beryl encouraged me to

216

climb with Catrin. She said when the girl first came that now I'd have someone to climb with.'

'I don't believe it.' Meshach shook his head doubtfully. 'Well, it could be true; she's a placid woman. She's put up with a lot in the past.'

'What are you on about now? And how do you come to know so much about my business?'

The old man regarded him sternly. 'I suppose you pretend it's all part of the job—the image, they call it: hard drinking, hard living, and the girls flocking after you in the pubs like sheep—under age too, many of them.'

'Of course, I'd forgotten you're pally with the police.'

'I don't listen to gossip—'

'You *what?*'

'—but your team don't hide its light under a bushel. There'd be a host of paternity orders against them if it wasn't the worst kind of girl uses the Commercial.'

'You're raving. To hear you talk no one would think you'd ever been young. My team's a bunch of normal chaps doing a bloody hard and dangerous job. And it's appreciated by most people. You've been listening to some impotent old flatfoot—your inspector friend probably—who's obsessed with envy because he's too old to get a woman for himself. My men aren't monks but I'll tell you something: they've got far more important things to think about than women. Saving lives is one. How they relax is their own business. They work hard and they play hard; do you think they're going to refuse what's offered them on a plate? You're talking like an old spinster.'

'You're trying to justify your own behaviour.'

'Oh, God! What I do is my own business. So's my relationship with my wife. Did you come here to meddle?'

'No. I've said nothing in twelve years—' this wasn't strictly true but he'd never made an issue of the subject until this moment, '—but the unfortunate thing is that you were climbing with the Massey girl on the day your lads were killed. That's why people are critical.'

'They've got to blame someone; they're vultures, pulling a carcass to bits.'

'You laid yourself wide open, boy.'

'Look,' Parry said tiredly: 'I had bad luck, that's all. How did I know the storm was going to be that bad? Keith completed his climb all right, no trouble. Who would have thought he'd suddenly take it into his head to stay out instead of coming down to the rendezvous?'

'That *was* bad luck,' his father agreed. 'There were a lot of coincidences, and all working against you.'

'I'm glad you appreciate it. I hope you also realise that I lost two of my men, and how I

218

feel about it.'

'I appreciate your feelings but aren't you forgetting the mothers? They've got feelings too. Keith was an only child.'

'Are you suggesting I was responsible?'

'You sent Gareth out that day.'

'You admitted it was bad luck—'

'Not bad luck that you weren't there; that was deliberate.'

'But wrong, you think?'

'I'm not judging you; you'll be judging yourself.'

'Then what *are* you doing? I asked you why you came. You haven't told me yet.'

'I don't like to see you in trouble.' Parry said nothing. The old man went on: 'I'd like to help if I can.'

'You're doing fine: first criticism, then blame.'

'I've told you how it looks to other people, and that was something that surprised you. You needed to know that; I doubt if Beryl would have said as much. And as for blame: if you've done wrong, it's you that has to live with it and try to remedy matters.'

'I made a mistake: putting the wrong man in charge in my absence. A boy—two boys—were killed. How do I remedy that?'

'You can't bring back the dead, but you could make a fresh start.'

Parry's eyes were bright with suspicion. 'Well, go on: tell me.'

'How about going away for a while?'

'Going *away*? You mean leave Minera? You said to remedy matters; that's making them worse: clearing out altogether.'

'You've got no choice now.'

'Bad as that, is it? You think I'll be lynched if I show my face in Minera? How quickly they can turn against you: like snakes.'

Meshach said evenly: 'I know that it will look as if you're running away but it could be that you've got to pay something for your mistake, and how people think of your leaving might be part of the price. It could be wise to go because of last weekend but that only brought things to a head, didn't it? You've not been yourself for a long time now; you're drinking too much, and there's these headaches: they're not natural in a man your age. Depressed, you are. Could be a new country and different people will work the trick; maybe you could start a rescue team in some place where it's needed badly, Scotland perhaps—you like Scotland.'

'I thought you sneered at rescue.'

'Not sneered, boy. I don't understand, but there: it's your life. What else can you do?'

Parry grinned without amusement. 'So you'll allow me rescue because I've got nothing else. Have you discussed this idea of leaving with Beryl?'

'Oh no; I'd speak to you first.'

'Well, you couldn't have spoken to her,

could you? When you were here yesterday people hadn't started talking.' He stared at the ceiling absently. 'At lunch time yesterday we hadn't found him.'

'I think you should go away,' Meshach said.

'You're driving me out too?'

'I only want to see you happy again, boy.'

CHAPTER FOURTEEN

When his father had gone Parry got up and started to prepare a meal for himself but the smell of frying bacon drove him outside retching miserably. By the time he'd forced down some dry toast and made a pot of tea it was nearly two o'clock. Remembering that the report had to be written, he put on his boots and anorak and walked to Hafod.

The flowers in Simon's garden were a battered tangle of stalks and limp blooms, looking even more dismal in the sunshine than they must have appeared during the storm.

Simon was working in the living room. He looked up at Parry's entrance but made no move to rise from his chair.

'I've come about the accident report,' Parry began.

'Oh yes. Having trouble with it?'

'I can't do it,' Parry said flatly.

Simon placed his pen in a glass tray. He

sighed. 'You want me to do it, I suppose.'

Parry looked at the table with its stacked books and the pad of paper with the top sheet half covered by a fine legible script.

'I've never asked you to do it before.'

'Why don't you ask Gareth to do it?'

'That wouldn't be very considerate in the circumstances.'

'It wouldn't, but if you won't do it, he's your obvious choice. I'm not a member of the team.'

'We don't have to bother with red tape. I'll sign it.'

'I'll do it—but only this time; I'm not the team's dogsbody.'

Parry sat down. Simon said meaningly: 'I'm working, Owen.'

'So I see. I'm sorry, but I can't go away while you're behaving like this. I'm—not feeling too good; Meshach came and found me in bed and I've just had all that I can take from him. He wants me to go away. Do you think I should?'

Simon looked at his notes. 'It's your life; don't get me to make your decisions for you.'

'I didn't think you'd be as unfriendly as this,' Parry said.

'Yes, well, it's a bit soon after last time, isn't it?'

'Meaning?'

Simon had been holding himself in check but Parry's obtuseness proved too much for

222

him. 'I mean coming up here for sympathy. The last time was only five days ago: the morning you came and were so shocked because Catrin had gone climbing with Keith. I wasted a lot of time feeling sorry for you then but you exploited that sympathy—and took all the rest of us for a ride—merely because you couldn't bear to lose Catrin to a younger man. I can understand straight jealousy, Owen, but what you did beats the band. You left here and went straight to the village and told Blodwen some cock-and-bull story about Keith being the great white hope of the team and that you wouldn't be interested in him if he was sacked from the garage. That was a dirty way to exploit Blodwen's loyalty to the boy; it was blackmail. And you'd already been to the garage and told Roberts to threaten Keith with the sack if he took another day off. You sealed every loophole: devious isn't in it—and for what a petty objective, just to keep two kids apart! You took Mollie to the Commercial and poured out some contrived problems to her and then—true to type—came out with the corny climax of suicide! But you took us all in; when Mollie came on the phone to me she was very worried. Severely depressed, she said you were: on the verge of a breakdown. Said we'd got to pull you out of it, and that if she and I couldn't, Catrin could.'

'I appreciated your help.'

'I bet you did. You even took Catrin in, and

223

she hasn't much time for failures in the normal way. God knows why she did it; she spent three days with you.'

'She enjoyed it.'

Simon shrugged. 'And that day you went to the Rhinogs: *the* Saturday: she knew it was going to blow like mad but she climbed just to humour you.'

'Where is she?'

'Out. As for Mollie: she's a trusting soul and you've disillusioned her completely. Last weekend was planned by you just to keep Catrin and Keith apart. You must have been mad!'

'I was.'

The other glared at him and asked with a kind of horrified wonder: 'You'd put the whole team at risk to keep a girl to yourself?'

Parry swallowed uncomfortably. 'I didn't think.'

'Good God! Does she realise what was in your mind?'

'She knows I stopped her climbing with the team deliberately. She accused me of it. I told her that I wanted to keep her to myself.'

'She told me that, but she didn't say you admitted as much. I've never known you go off the deep end over a girl before; what's got into you?'

'You told me: middle-age.'

'You're infatuated. She's leaving next week and she doesn't give a damn about you.'

'I'm leaving too.'

'Not with her—'

'I'm going to Scotland.'

Simon looked at him suspiciously. 'When?'

'Some time. There's a few things to wind up here. Beryl will have to give in her notice and since we pay rent in advance—'

'You're leaving for good?'

'Why not? There's nothing for me here.'

'Don't wallow in it, man; you think too much about yourself. You never give a thought to other people. Look at that boy.'

'What boy?'

'Why, the one whose father died on Craig y Castell. When did you last ring the hospital about him?'

'I've forgotten.'

'You would. I rang this morning; he's off the danger list.'

'Good.' Parry caught the other's eye and shrugged. 'I can't feel involved: it's just a bit of information you've given me, not a life I've saved. No—' as the other gestured in annoyance, '—I'm not asking for sympathy, I'm telling you. You said I was a shit and you're right; my whole bloody life's been a sham—'

'Don't start on that,' Simon warned, then cocked his head, listening. 'Here's a car.'

They waited, Simon avoiding the other's eyes. The latch of the gate clicked, there were steps on the path and Mollie appeared. She

225

stopped in the doorway when she saw Parry, then came in slowly. She looked from him to Simon.

'Owen came to tell me he's moving to Scotland,' the big man said in the awkward silence.

'Oh.' She turned to Parry. 'Is Beryl going too?'

'Of course.'

'Well, pastures new and all that.'

Parry coughed. 'I want to apologise for that scene in the Commercial.'

'Forget it.' Her face was stiff with embarrassment. 'If you've been justifying your behaviour to Simon, he doesn't want to go through it a second time—and I'm not interested.'

'I'll call at your place for my book,' Parry said.

She bit her lip and her eyes were suddenly bright. She made a helpless gesture towards Simon who regarded Parry balefully. She said: 'It's not the one action I find so unforgivable, Owen, but the bloody stupid mess you've made of things. You had everything going for you and you threw it all up for a senile infatuation. Why couldn't you play it her way and keep it cool?' She doesn't give a damn for men—no, you keep quiet, Simon—she just picks them up and discards them like Parry with his tarts in the Commercial.'

'You're not being fair to Catrin,' Simon said

226

hotly. 'She was sorry for him.'

'Oh, I agree; I'm not angry with Catrin, I'm appalled at the waste of a good man—three men,' she added softly: 'I was fond of Keith. He was so *vital*.' She went on bitterly to Parry: 'You didn't know what was going to happen with the team when you abandoned them but I don't expect you gave it a thought: that anything could happen. All you were thinking of was your own selfish ends.' She put her hands to her mouth. 'Hell, I didn't mean to say all this . . .'

'My book,' Parry reminded her without expression.

Her face was ugly with despair. 'I must leave it to you after all,' she told him heavily. 'My heart's not in it now. Take it out when you've been away for some time and re-read it. There's a good story in it.' She sounded forlorn.

'You might get a book from one of the lads,' he told her.

'Yes.' She brightened. 'I've seen Gareth's personal log of rescues. It's very good—a book in the making, in fact. I should have known he could do it: he's competent at English, articulate, humane.' There was an edge to her voice.

'I see.' Then he said, as if he were merely politely curious: 'And I suppose he's going to run the team.'

'He's the obvious choice.'

Parry regarded her steadily. 'Chosen before anyone knew I was leaving,' he remarked, as if to himself. 'Will he be able to keep discipline or will he lose another man next weekend?' His tone was interested, academic. Mollie frowned and glanced at Simon. 'I'd rather you were the leader,' Parry told the big man. 'But you won't do it, will you? You're quite right to keep clear of it; a guy's got to go to the top and when he gets there, there's nowhere to go but down.' He grinned horribly. 'Proof. Here's me: a few days ago I was the Golden Boy and Gareth was the Boy Scout. Now Gareth's where I was and I'm dirt. I'm being run out of the district.' He frowned. 'I still don't see how it happened. I mean, *he* killed those boys, not me.' He looked at Simon. 'You said to delegate—'

'Oh no!' Simon exclaimed. 'Don't try and shift the blame to me!'

'I don't know what happened,' Parry repeated. His head was throbbing abominably and he leaned forward and held it in both hands, gasping with the pain.

Mollie was saying coldly: 'It's no good getting hysterical about it. Gareth blames himself and he hasn't said a word against you and never will. He didn't kill those lads; they didn't know their navigation and the storm was too much for them. Keith gave up, Owen; he hadn't the guts to go on. There wasn't a mark on him; he just panicked quietly and sat down

228

to die. Gareth feels responsible because he couldn't impose his authority on Keith, but then Keith wasn't good team material; if he'd come down safely on Saturday, he'd have come to grief eventually. As for you: you've had your time with the team; now you've got to give way to a younger man. It's the old herd bull business—but Gareth didn't even have to contest the leadership with you; you abdicated.'

'He's not well,' Simon put in. 'What's the matter, Owen?'

'My head's blinding me . . . headache.'

Simon blundered out of the room and returned with aspirins and water. He watched with concern as Parry gulped the tablets.

'You'd better see a doctor,' he said. 'You look dreadful.'

*   *   *

He left Hafod and walked up the track to the road-end where he lay on the turf and closed his eyes. He must have slept because when he opened them again the sun had moved round and the shadows were lengthening across the combe. He looked at the path zig-zagging down the headwall and saw a new picture—except that it was a week old: Keith dropping down through the bracken with all the lovely carelessness of youth. He closed his eyes and looked again: it had been a trick of the light.

Catrin was running down the path. He felt the dread of yet another encounter steal over him and remembered Meshach's warning of the price he would have to pay.

He knew the moment when she caught sight of him because she checked, didn't quite stop, and then continued delicately like a wary hind. She approached without greeting him and halted to regard him with the same cool interest which she'd shown on the first occasion that he saw her: looking at a body.

'Have you been waiting long?'

'Waiting?'

She bit her lip, then smiled. *'Touché.* I thought you were waiting for me.'

'I was at Simon's. I came up here for some air. The valley seems a bit close today.'

'You mustn't take any notice of Simon. Mollie and he have been working each other up. They're remarkably high-principled where rescue is concerned. They were going at it last night like a couple of ham actors. I went to bed. What's the matter? You look like a fish out of water. Has everyone been jumping down your throat today?'

'Don't you care? I mean, about the weekend?'

She sat down on the grass beside him. 'Look; how many times do people make mistakes and get away with it—until something disastrous happens and they're caught out? It's like climbing: you must have done the wrong thing scores of times—and recovered yourself before anything serious happened. But if you hadn't recovered yourself and been killed, you could have been called incompetent at the least, and if other men died as a result of your mistakes, people would say, privately, that you were a monster. So you made a mistake in going to the Rhinogs; it was your bad luck that you got caught. If there'd been no accident, your men would have had *more* respect for you because you dropped them in favour of a girl. That's how they'd see it.'

'They'd be wrong,' he said, 'but so long as no harm came from it, what they thought wouldn't matter.'

'Does it matter now?' The question rendered him speechless. 'Well, I see it does,' she went on with some impatience. 'That's parochial attitudes for you. What can you do about it?'

'I'm pulling out.'

'You are? Where are you going?'

'To Scotland.' Reluctantly but with compulsion he added: 'If you don't want me to go to Australia with you.'

She shook her head. 'Nothing doing. We're the proverbial ships passing in the night, you and I.'

'You asked Keith to go.'

'How did you know that?'

'Blodwen told me.'

'I didn't mean it.'

231

He nodded. 'He never knew you were taking him for a ride so his last days must have been pleasant with the adventure ahead—' she made to interrupt but he went on evenly: 'The tragedy of it is that I thought you were planning to take him away. I believed you could do it. That's why I was so careful to see that Keith was occupied that weekend: to stop him coming to look for you. That's why I went so far away that I wasn't on hand to search for him in the daylight on Saturday.'

'I knew they'd got it wrong,' she said. 'Simon's convinced you're in love with me.'

He raised tired eyelids. 'I should have let you climb with the team and taken Keith to the Rhinogs.' He smiled weakly. 'But he wouldn't have come.'

' "Should have", "ought to have done"! Do you spend your life regretting your mistakes?'

'Not until now.'

'You must have loved him very much.'

He sat absolutely still until the tears brimmed over and ran down his cheeks, when he wiped his face clumsily with his hands. 'Perhaps he was taking the place of a son with me,' he said at last.

'It doesn't matter.'

'What doesn't?'

'How it was. It's your Puritan streak coming out and all this hell-fire religion. The Welsh are so full of guilt, poor things. You're killing yourself trying to live up to your wolfish

232

reputation and all the time women disgust you. It's *that* behaviour which is perverted, not being in love with another chap.'

'I wasn't—' He stopped and studied her for what seemed a long time but her expression remained cool and kind and totally uncomprehending.

He stood up. 'When did you guess?' he asked as if it were of no importance.

'When you looked at me across his body. Does anyone else know?'

He shook his head and managed a smile. 'All Minera thinks I'm infatuated with you. Ironic, isn't it?'

'Life's like that. Good-bye.'

*   *   *

From the summit of Craig y Castell he watched the moon-glow spread beyond the pinnacles across the combe. It was so still he could hear a flight of curlews winging their way to the winter feeding grounds where the river met the sea, and piping as they went.

Below him the gully dropped to the heather ledge above eight hundred feet of space. He knew where the snags were. From this place one might lodge in the gully and live a long time; one might, like the boy who came out of the coma, survive. The correct place was from the heather ledge some fifteen feet south of the gully; below that was Lacewing, and below

Lacewing there were still two-thirds of the face to go.

He moved round the cairn and settled himself facing away from the cliff and looking down the dark bulk of the peninsula that stretched to the island where ten thousand saints were buried. How did they find space for so many on that tiny speck of rock? Perhaps saints took up less room.

His head hadn't ached since that terrible spasm at Hafod. It was tension that made it worse, that much was obvious. A sedentary occupation? He grinned. He was sedentary enough for the time that was left to him. He felt relaxed. Was this an intrinsic mood immediately prior to death or had his subconscious mind taken a decision and ruled out conflict? But if his subconscious had decided, he'd be forced to go down to the ledge: the conscious mind would be overruled. On the other hand could such serenity be associated with life rather than death? If he decided to live—providing the decision was still open to him—could he recapture this mood? Obviously he would lose it as soon as he returned to Cwm Daron. To find it again if only occasionally would be worth living for. He thought of Scotland and the gaunt white peaks shouldering away to the horizon, of toppling sea stacks and wheeling birds.

He thought of these things carefully, with concentration, and discovered that, whereas a few days ago he had tried to picture old delights but had been able to summon them only as facts with no emotional depth, now when he thought of them what came to mind was not the tangible mountain, but the feel of it: of stillness, of beauty, of untrammelled peace. And so he turned, objectively, to the thought of death.

It appeared that there was no point in killing himself if there was some reason, any reason, to go on living, for the heart of the matter was not that he wanted to die but that he had no further interest in life. In view of this there had seemed no alternative but to give up, particularly as he was finding that those occasions were on the increase when life became actively distasteful.

However, at this moment, sitting on the summit of Craig y Castell, struck suddenly by the wonder that the moon rose without sound, then listening but catching only the call of a laggard curlew, it occurred to him, if only because he felt the loneliness of the bird and could listen for the moon, that there was a reason for living.

The deep channel of concentration, more powerful than that required on rock, carried him inexorably to the other side, to consider his fall and extinction. He knew that the initial action, although devoid of suffering and horror, although requiring great courage, was, because of that last factor, unreasonable and useless behaviour. The direction was to live. Living would, of course, demand more courage, but then that could be another reason for not dying. In one brief moment, so fleeting that it made no impression on his brain, it was borne in on him that the courage factor might be the best motive for staying alive.

CHAPTER FIFTEEN

The sun woke him and to judge from its position it was midday. There had been a touch of frost during the night and he could smell the rime melting as the warmth reached it.

He'd arrived home late, hurrying down the track, worried that Beryl might have become anxious at his long absence. If she had gone up to Hafod and Catrin had told her that he'd set out for the tops in the early evening, would she have speculated on his state of mind?

There had been a light in Hafod but he hadn't wanted to face more of Simon's hostility so he went on, meaning to ring from Dolwen if Beryl was not there. But she was there; she'd left a light in the kitchen and when he went upstairs and listened in the doorway of the bedroom, he could hear her breathing.

She'd stirred when he came to bed but she hadn't wakened. She was big and warm and comfortable to touch and he fell asleep immediately.

He was ravenously hungry when he woke and he couldn't remember when he'd last eaten. After the experience of yesterday morning he didn't attempt to fry bacon but ate eggs and toast. Afterwards he cleared the table, washed his breakfast dishes, made the bed and laid the fire, then went outside and started to put the rescue equipment in order. There was a host of small jobs to do and these he set about methodically. It took him some time and when he'd finished he made an inventory of the equipment and of all the gear that was out on loan to the team members.

When Beryl came home from work he was typing the list at the kitchen table. Her appearance startled him and he looked at his watch.

'Why didn't you give me a ring?' he asked. 'I'd have come and fetched you.' He got up and put the kettle on.

'How are you feeling?' Beryl asked, hanging her coat on the door.

'Much better, thanks. Did you worry about me last night?'

'No. Why?'

He was surprised and embarrassed. 'Well, you left me in bed in the morning—and then I was out all evening without leaving a note. I thought you might wonder where I was.'

She looked surprised herself. 'You never

leave notes—not when you go out for an evening. I thought you were at Hafod, or at the Commercial with the team.'

'But I didn't take the—' He stopped, realising that she hadn't looked to see if the Land Rover was in its shed. He fetched mugs and milk, moving slowly, bewildered. She seemed to have no conception of the devastating effect the weekend's events had made on him: that visiting at Hafod and drinking with the boys, was part of a past life, an alien world. He wondered how she had escaped the gossip.

'I was out walking,' he said carelessly as he made the tea.

'Oh, you weren't at Hafod?'

So she thought he'd been with Catrin.

'I was alone on the tops.' He smiled. 'I wanted to be on my own—and the moon was almost full.'

'It must have been lovely up there.'

'Yes,' he agreed feelingly. 'It was. I enjoyed myself.'

'I'm so glad.' She sounded as if she meant it. He brought her tea and she sat down with a sigh of relief. 'Oh, you've laid the fire.'

He shrugged. 'I got up late but I've done quite a bit since.'

She glanced at the table but didn't ask what he was writing. He appreciated that because it meant that the question of the report and therefore of the accident was a subject which

238

she would leave to him to raise.

'I'm copying out an inventory of the equipment,' he told her.

'Hadn't you got one already?'

'Not up to date, and I need one now particularly.' She looked at him sharply and his eyes gleamed. 'Beryl, how would you feel about going to Scotland?'

Her initial astonishment was followed by an expression which he couldn't fathom, but it wasn't delight. He was not surprised; he'd known it would be a wrench for her to leave Minera after so long. She had her job here, her friends—and there was Meshach. She'd think of his being left on his own, and there was the problem of finding a house in Scotland.

'Are you serious?' she asked.

'Oh yes, I'm quite decided.' He looked away. 'Gareth will be taking over the team.'

'Have you seen him?'

'No, Mollie told me yesterday.'

'It's terribly sudden . . .'

'It's been building up for a long time, but Scotland was Meshach's idea. I didn't need to think about it for long though. It's better that we should leave; people are hostile after last weekend. They blame me for the accident.'

She wasn't surprised. 'They wouldn't mention it to me,' she said and then, after a pause: 'Gareth blames himself.'

He ignored this last. 'It looks as if I'm running away,' he admitted, 'but it's the logical thing to do. I should have got out long before this weekend; I was going stale in Minera.'

'I've known for some time that you weren't happy.'

'So,' he went on, 'how about it? We can stay with the MacIntyres—' these were climbing friends, '—at Fort William until we find somewhere to live, store the furniture in their barn, and I'll look around. I can think of several places where they could do with a rescue team; all I've got to do is spend a few days in each area that I have in mind: find out how many able-bodied chaps I could get together, look at houses . . . Of course, there'd need to be some kind of work near for you.' He laughed deprecatingly. 'That sounds as if I mean to exploit you, but you do want to work, don't you?' She made a small gesture which he took for assent and he rattled on: 'You'll love Scotland; suppose we went to the Cairngorms where the climate's much better than on the west coast—or perhaps you'd prefer to be near the sea—?' His eyes were anxious. Still she didn't respond. 'Well,' he continued, feeling a trifle deflated: 'Would you like me to get a job, part-time perhaps—or even full-time—' his pace quickened again: 'There are heaps of big estates in the Cairngorms: rich landowners who'll pay well; some of them are bound to need a handyman, or even an estate manager. After all, other team leaders manage to hold down a nine-to-five job and run a team; there's

240

no reason why I shouldn't be able to do it, no reason at all. If I had a job you could stay at home—and perhaps then—' He stopped, remembering the last time he'd raised the question of adoption, or rather, of children.

'You're very enthusiastic,' she said at last.

'Of course I am. I'm raring to go!'

'Would you go on your own?'

He gaped at her, then he understood. 'I see; you've put down roots. Yes, I know it's difficult to make a move at our age but I can't stay—now. It isn't so much the village gossip, that would die down in time particularly as Catrin's leaving this week, but I've lost the team—and Simon and Mollie: they've turned against me.'

'Because of Catrin?'

'Not really: because of what happened to Keith—and Deri. They blame me for not being there, you see. They think I should have put the team first. That's where Gareth wins; he made a mistake but he *was* with the team.'

'Catrin's going to Australia,' Beryl said.

'I know.'

'Wouldn't you want to go with her?'

'You're too damned accommodating, woman. I don't want Catrin; I want you.' She raised her eyebrows. 'You're thinking about last week,' he continued heavily. 'That's all over. I never had any feeling for her anyway; she's heartless and stupid. Don't look at me like that! It's true. I'm not in love with her.'

'You were just carried away?'

241

'Not that either,' he said grimly.

'If you call her heartless it does rather sound as if she's given you the brush-off.'

'It's not important. If you must know: she asked Keith to go with her to Australia but told me that she never meant it. Blodwen told me that Keith took it seriously, but since he never found out, it's not important.'

'It wouldn't have meant much to him if he had found out; kids recover quickly from disappointments.'

'He wasn't a kid. We all think of him as one but that's because we're old.' He didn't want to talk about Keith. He got up to fetch the teapot. When he returned he said: 'I don't like you being so casual about me and Catrin; it's as if you were pushing me at her.'

'I thought you enjoyed climbing with her.' She was prevaricating.

'Didn't you mind me going with her?'

'You asked me that the other night and I told you that I did mind. I thought she'd hurt you. She seemed ruthless. She's looking for a man: a certain man, and when she finds him she'll be warm enough but until then she'll pick men up and toss them aside when she finds they don't suit her.'

'You've summed her up—but when you asked me if I didn't want to go away with her, wasn't that a bit risky if you thought I was infatuated?'

Beryl picked at her skirt. 'It could be that I

242

wanted to get things clear.'

'Well, now you know. Catrin's out of my life and I don't care if I have to meet her again; it won't be painful.'

'I'm glad of that.'

'Now we understand each other. So you see, going to Scotland has nothing to do with her. You can be perfectly sure I'm not pining for anyone—' a shadow crossed his face, '—it will make it easier to bear last weekend though, to forget it in time.'

'Yes,' she said softly. 'That must be hard.'

'Well, how soon can we go?' he asked on a false note.

Her face changed. 'I asked if you'd go alone, Owen.'

'Not without you,' he said firmly. 'Think about it for a while; you'll get used to the idea. They have Women's Institutes there, you know, and you're the sort of person who will fit in anywhere. You'll be glad we went once we've found a house. This is a poky hole.' He looked round the room disparagingly.

'I'm not going.' Her tone should have warned him but he ignored it and returned to his theme: 'You'll come round once things start moving; I'll go and see the colonel tomorrow and give him notice about this place—'

'I can't go!' Now he caught the desperate note in her voice.

'What? Why *can't* you go?'

243

She looked at him sadly. 'I *was* pushing—no, not that—I was hoping you were in love with Catrin. I did think she was wrong for you but I thought you'd quarrel when you were thousands of miles away, and split up, and you wouldn't come back. You'd have stayed out there and got some kind of a job—' she smiled wanly, '—started a team in the Himalayas—'

'What is all this? You wanted to get rid of me? Why, for God's sake? Are you sick of me?'

'No, I'm not sick of you—but didn't you ever wonder, when you were running after girls, or afterwards, didn't you ever give a thought to me?'

'I did, and I've felt guilty as hell sometimes—' this wasn't true but it was an easy lie, '—but I've always come back to you; none of them was ever *serious.*'

'I didn't mean that. I meant didn't you ever think I might have feelings: that I might fall in love?'

He gasped and leaned back in his chair. He started to smile and then wiped it off; she wasn't joking. Poor old Beryl. He wondered if it was usual for women to be like this when they were going through the change.

'No,' he said sympathetically, 'I didn't know you felt like that.'

'But women have sexual urges too.'

'You should have told me.'

'And they want to be loved, although I have

244

to admit it wasn't deliberate. I didn't welcome it, but I suppose I did slide into it rather too easily.'

He sighed, wondering how long this would last, wondering if she'd get worse. He used to have fantasies when he was in the back of the 'Rover with the village tarts, pretending they were clean and kind and intelligent, but his wife had had nothing else but fantasies. It was a long time since he'd made love to her.

'How long have you felt like this?' he asked.

She frowned. 'It started last winter.'

'I see.' It was like making a diagnosis, asking the patient where the pain was. 'Have you been to the doctor?'

She started and looked at him wide-eyed. He could see the thoughts racing behind her eyes and he remembered then that it would be a psychiatrist in a case like this, not an ordinary doctor. He'd frightened her, he thought.

'You don't believe me,' she said and smiled ruefully. 'You think I'm making it up.'

'No, dear. Who is it?'

'It's Gareth.'

He pondered this and thought it was logical. It would have to be either Simon or Gareth; they both liked her but she'd been thrown into Gareth's company more because she did the refreshments at the youth club—and then he brought her home.

'Does he know how you feel?' he asked.

'Owen, you've got to face it: I'm telling you the truth!'

'So, you've been having an affair with Gareth and you don't want to come to Scotland because that will take you away from him, is that it?'

'We want to get married,' she said dully.

'I'll tell you what we'll do,' he said kindly, as if he were talking to a child: 'We'll go to Scotland and I'll get a proper job and you can stay at home. Then we'll adopt not one baby but several; kids without parents, that need a lot of love. Do it to please me, eh?'

'No, Owen.'

'But you want a family; I know you do.'

'Yes, but I want my own.'

'Well that's out, isn't it?' he said roughly. 'So we'll adopt.'

'It's not out; I'm going to have a child.'

He couldn't cope with her; he needed expert help. 'And I suppose you've been to the doctor,' he said, at the end of his tether. When he'd said that before, she'd been startled. He'd got there too quickly.

'I'm three months pregnant.'

'So it's not mine.'

'No, Gareth is the father.'

*   *   *

The surgery wasn't crowded and he had to wait only twenty minutes to see the doctor. He was

246

the last patient. The doctor had just received a call. 'If it's not urgent, Parry . . .'

'It's about my wife—Beryl—she's been to see you?'

The other took it as a statement, not a question. 'Yes, yes; last week.'

'I don't think she's at all well, I wanted to ask you—'

The doctor was checking his bag. He stopped and looked over his glasses at the other. 'All you middle-aged fellows are the same; there's nothing to worry about, Parry! She's a bit old for a first but she's fine and healthy and she's got a good broad body for childbearing. I can see your point; after all these years you can't believe that she's got the same organs as a younger woman, but I examined her very thoroughly and I assure you everything's going to be all right.' He put a hand on Parry's shoulder and steered him to the door. 'I'll be keeping an eye on her of course, but nothing's going to go wrong—why, with a pelvis like that, your wife could be presenting you with twins in six months' time! Now you run along and have a whisky with the boys to celebrate—and see you take care on those mountains!' Chuckling, he went back along the passage to the surgery leaving Parry on his own.

CHAPTER SIXTEEN

At Bryn Mawr the Graingers were in the kitchen, eating supper with their backs to the window. There was a television set on the sideboard and they were watching a Western which was building up to a climax. The labrador was stretched in front of the stove.

Parry retreated from the window and went round the house, treading softly.

The side door wasn't bolted. He let himself in and walked along the passage to the gun room. He'd been here before, at a time when the colonel had been trying to interest him in shooting. He took a shotgun and some cartridges and left by the way he'd come. He didn't glance in the kitchen as he passed; he could hear the screen battle in progress through the closed window.

The Land Rover was parked below the rhododendrons. He got in, placed the gun on the seat and drove back to the village.

Gareth lived alone in the house which had belonged to his parents: a cottage at the end of a side street. Parry parked at the kerb, loaded the gun and, holding it close to his body, knocked on the door. When it was opened he pushed past Gareth into the living room. The First Aider turned, puzzled by the lack of greeting, then stiffened.

248

Parry regarded him steadily, holding the gun with the barrels pointing at the other's chest.

Gareth's forehead was shining. 'Take a seat?' he said, as if it were a question.

There was a chair behind the other but he didn't sit down.

'What good will it do?' Gareth asked hopelessly.

'You should have thought of that before. You didn't think of the consequences of your actions, did you?' It was meant as a sneer but it came out with a note of desperation.

'Does anyone?' Gareth looked at the gun and frowned. 'I didn't know you cared for her that much.'

'She was all I had left,' Parry said.

The other man considered this, putting his hand absently on the back of a kitchen chair.

'Don't throw that,' Parry warned. 'This thing's loaded.'

'You've had a hell of a lot of shocks these last few days,' Gareth said thoughtfully. 'Did it start with the boy on Craig y Castell? Yes,' he answered himself softly, 'it could have been that. You were upset by the father dying—and then it was you who found the son. But you did a good job getting him down . . .?' Again there was that rising inflection, as if he were asking a question. 'Then there was this weekend . . . but killing me won't wipe that out, nor the other.' Alarm showed in his eyes. 'Is Beryl all right?'

'I haven't touched her. I didn't believe her.'

'It's true.'

'I know. I've seen the doctor.'

'I see. So there's that too.'

'All these years,' Parry said, 'we didn't have a child, and I've looked at the girls I've had, and seen them pushing prams and thought I was filling Minera with bastards and that it was just my luck to marry a barren woman and now—this.'

'It might be just a simple matter—'

'Don't give me that! I'm sterile—no better than a bloody bullock.'

Gareth shook his head. 'You've done a man's job for twelve years—with the team,' he added quickly. 'I enjoyed working with you.'

'Yeah, *with* me, not under me. I was the leader but you've always wanted my place.'

'I had my job,' Gareth said. 'Did you want it? You didn't like dealing with bad wounds.'

'You do? You like violence. You've got it now.' The gun lifted, pointing at the other's eyes.

Gareth said firmly: 'I hate violence; that's why I did the First Aid course. I can't bear to watch suffering so I have to do something to try to lessen it.'

'You were always different,' Parry said viciously. 'Always trying to undermine my authority.'

'You've got undisputed authority with the men, and you know it. You're apparently ruthless and that's what they like; it's how you

250

control them. You hold that team together; they think they're hard but they're a bunch of sheep without you.'

'They can stand on their own,' Parry rejoined automatically.

'They'd go to pieces without a leader.'

'And you think you can lead them.'

'No. I can take over with your authority behind me but, God knows, I've made a hash of it now. My job's with the youth club: preparing boys for the team, and my lads can't wait for the day when they're working under you.'

'You should have had a fatality before this,' Parry told him: 'Taking bunches of boys on the hill with only one leader.'

'You've got to take risks; it's a dangerous game.'

'A game?' The gun jerked.

'Pursuit, then.'

'The luck's been all on your side.'

'Not for twelve years; no one could be lucky all that time. My boys couldn't have been incompetent when you took them on as probationers or you wouldn't have accepted them.'

'I licked them into shape. Keith was in your club for a while; why wasn't he any good at navigation?'

'He wasn't too bad but he was at the age when all they want to do is climb; they're not interested in anything else. Why navigation? It wasn't that that killed him.'

'What was it then?' Parry felt for the chair with one hand. and sat down. Gareth watched the gun which was still covering him. 'It was a combination of circumstances,' he said. 'Perhaps he took the wrong bearing on top of Carnedd Iago. He's navigated with the team when we've been in mist but it's different when you're in a crowd; there's always someone to check if you make a mistake.'

'He wasn't alone on Saturday,' Parry pointed out. 'He was with Deri.'

'Deri was a bit thick when it came to map reading—and with that pair Keith would be the dominant one. That was where I made my big mistake. Now if it had been Idris Evans with Keith, Idris wouldn't have gone wrong on the Skyline Route, but then Keith couldn't have persuaded him not to go straight back to Hafod from the summit.'

'Do you think Keith persuaded Deri to go round the Skyline?'

'That's the way I reckon it was. Keith was the one who was full of enthusiasm, but he hadn't enough experience; he wasn't ready to cope with emergencies like that storm.'

'Mollie says he'd have come to grief eventually anyway; that he wasn't suitable for the team.'

'She knows nothing about it.' Gareth moved and sat down on the kitchen chair. 'I think we could have made a good mountaineer out of

Keith. After all, everyone makes mistakes; we weren't better than him because we survived, just luckier.' Parry stared at him. 'I mean,' Gareth went on: 'We were at his standard once, weren't we?'

'But—that bit about him sitting down and just waiting to die: he didn't have much guts, did he?'

Parry's eyes pleaded and Gareth regarded him gravely. 'It's all a matter of experience— and the precise moment at which you know panic for the first time.'

'He panicked?'

'*You* haven't? Never? Yes, and so have I. I was alone, coming up to Carnedd Iago with the light going, thick cloud and a covering of snow. Then the cloud parted and I couldn't recognise a bloody thing. I was utterly desolate. The cloud came back and I couldn't move.'

'Where were you?'

'I'd gone off that ridge to the north; I was on the pass above Cwm Caseg. I've never had to fight so hard since to hang on to my sanity. Just a matter of concentration, people would say who didn't know, but it isn't, is it? It's a struggle with demons. *You* know. How much chance would there have been for me if it hadn't been a still evening? And the storm that Keith had wasn't an ordinary gale.'

'Then why did Deri go on?'

'Deri had less imagination and probably

more stamina and, if he couldn't persuade Keith to continue, someone had to go for help.'

'He should have stayed—Is that what you told his mother?'

'Yes.'

'I see.' Parry looked unhappy. They were silent for a few moments, then he went on: 'We ought to take them out in bad weather more often: in small groups—even send them out alone, do you think?' He shifted in his chair and reached over to lean the gun carefully against the side of the fireplace.

'We could have checkpoints on the tops,' Gareth said: 'To keep careful track of them. The first thing to do would be to send them out in pairs.'

'Means a lot more work. In winter too; we have a call-out about one weekend in every two.'

'We'd have to consider it carefully.' Gareth gestured to the table. 'I'm working on a course of navigation lectures now—for evenings, of course, not for the weekend.'

'You're taking over the team,' Parry said flatly.

'That's in Mollie's mind too. Why should I?'

'I'm leaving.'

'You're resigning?'

'I'm going to Scotland.'

'You don't have to leave. I've applied for a job in Birmingham.'

'You'd have gone and left Beryl?'

'Oh no.' His voice was steady. 'I wouldn't have left her.'

'So she'd have gone with you.' Parry said heavily, staring at the floor. 'I don't think I love her; I'm very *fond* of her—when it's too late. Last night it was the thought of her brought me home—at least,' he amended, 'it was one of the things that brought me down: my marriage.'

'What happened last night?'

'I went up to Craig y Castell to throw myself off the top.'

'Good God!'   Gareth stared at him in amazement. 'Did you tell her that?'

'No.'

'But you came back to try to persuade her to stay with you after all, is that it?'

'You've got it wrong. Beryl didn't tell me about you till tonight. I told you I didn't believe her.'

'Then what made you go up to Craig y Castell last night?'

'It was the weekend. No, it was more than that, but his death put the lid on it—or opened the lid. Simon said that rescuers have to keep compassion in a box, although I don't think it was compassion I had for Keith. How could it have been—with him? After he was killed, yes, but not before.'

'You were fond of him.'

'Yes.' Parry was expressionless.

Gareth nodded. 'He was a lovable lad. Thought a lot of you too.'

' "Lovable"?' There was awe in Parry's voice but Gareth misunderstood him.

'Yes. I taught him, don't forget that; perhaps it was because of knowing him so well that I could see past the wildness—but who actually disliked him? He wasn't a hooligan; there was no malice about him. All Keith needed was an outlet. He got that with the team. He was a happy boy at school but in the team he bloomed. What's the matter? You look puzzled.'

Parry said carefully, 'I hadn't realised he was a favourite with you as well.'

'He had to be. The rest of the team was bovine beside Keith.'

'Yes. I showed my feelings when we found him, so Catrin Massey thinks I'm queer.'

'What's queer about—? Oh. You mean she thinks you're homosexual?'

'That's right.'

'And you value her opinion. She's not really like that; it's just a pose.'

'Like what?'

'Why, that hard sophisticated shell: never showing her feelings, unshockable. She must have been hurt some time, and badly; she must have been because she's so terrified of being hurt again. Catrin's armour-plated, surely you realised that?'

'I thought she was cold.'

'No, just frightened of men—of people really. I see it with some kids in school. Now Keith was just the opposite: plunging into every experience that came his way; you were bound to be fascinated by him—particularly you.'

'Now what—?'

Gareth smiled. 'Catrin's brainwashed you. I mean you would be more attracted to Keith than most because you'd admire his courage. You keep yourself on too tight a rein: scared of showing your feelings.'

Parry looked very tired. Gareth asked wonderingly: '*Was* Keith homosexual? Bisexual? It never showed in school.'

'Not that I know of.'

'I see. But you were worried about being attracted to him—is that it?'

Parry's eyes were appealing in the ravaged face. 'He was the only person I've ever loved; never a girl. When it came it had to be a boy. What could I think?'

'And you kept it quiet.'

'I couldn't even think about it.'

'You've been in hell. There was guilt, I suppose, and horror?' Parry nodded dumbly. 'Then you came to hate yourself—and probably much more at the weekend.'

'It was the sex side of it,' Parry confessed. 'Catrin slept with him so I thought my jealousy was because I wanted him like that too—'

'Did you?'

257

'No.'

'Christ! What a bloody world we live in! Didn't it ever occur to you that parents get possessive in the same way when their children bring home friends of the opposite sex? It *is* sex, but so what? What does it matter? We live with it.' Gareth grinned hugely. 'None of it was doing any harm, Owen; the harm was in your mind, in what you were doing to yourself. The only sin was guilt.'

'Now is a good time to tell me.'

The other's face fell. 'I'm sorry.' He looked up and said quietly: 'But when it happens again, you'll remember what we've said.' His tone changed to one of frank curiosity. 'What made you decide not to kill yourself?'

'Ah,' Parry said: *'Then?* But I got it over for good. I've thought about it for a long time; as all the things I set a value on seemed to be slipping away: enjoying things, having fun. Climbing, drinking, birds. But,' he added softly, 'I never did enjoy them. I was afraid of suicide. I used to plan it but I knew I'd never have the courage to carry it through. So I climbed to my limit, hoping that the decision would be taken out of my hands, and when I pushed over the limit and ought to have been killed, I found I was fighting like hell to stay alive. I was terrified of death. And I was bored with life. As you said: I hated myself. Then, this last week, everything went: Keith, my reputation, Simon, Mollie. I didn't know I'd lost Beryl as well, not last night. I had the courage last night but it was the moon that stopped me, and the stillness. If it had been a wild night I would have done it.'

'No,' Gareth said. 'The moon gave you a chance to relax. You couldn't have done that on a wild night but you would have fought again: struggling with demons on the top of Craig y Castell. And then you'd have come down and had to sweat it out for another session until the moment came when you'd win finally.'

Parry smiled. 'You think it's final.'

'Isn't it?'

'I'm not a potential suicide—but I don't kid myself that life's going to be a bed of roses.'

They both looked at the shotgun. Parry said: 'I'm *not* a suicide but I had to go up there to find that out. I'm not a killer either but something made me come here with a gun instead of spending the rest of my life wishing I'd killed you, thinking I ought to have done.'

'Civilised demons,' Gareth said.

'I've always hated you.' Parry was quietly conversational. 'You're a better man than I am—no—' as the other made to interrupt, '— not a better *rescuer.* I'll go to Scotland and form a team that will knock yours into a cocked hat.'

'I don't know if I can hold them together without you,' Gareth said doubtfully.

'Take advantage of my unpopularity, man.

259

Wade in!'

'Stop crucifying yourself. You're a hero to them.'

'A hero! I'm the world's worst coward. Whenever anything gets hard, I'm all knotted inside. That's why you have to do the First Aid; it made me sick to call on you for that: a job I couldn't do. I would have given anything to be callous. You say I was ruthless with the men—'

'*Apparently* ruthless.'

Parry shot him a glance. 'Are you apparently callous with the victims?'

'If callousness means unmoved, yes.'

'But you feel for them, really?'

Gareth frowned. 'I did at first—but it's a matter of training yourself. What can you do for them if you're concerned with their suffering—if you get involved? You've got to keep your mind clear and objective; you have to think of arteries and organs and the rate of the fellow's pulse. If you're distracted by moans and the fear your own men are feeling at the time, how can you concentrate? For me pain has to be physical only: something to guide me in a diagnosis. How do *you* feel with bad injuries, when you have to deal with them?'

'I hated them. I had to hate the victims. It was all I could do. If I hadn't done that, I'd have sat down and cried with the agony of it all. Do you see?'

Before Gareth could reply there was a sudden loud knocking at the door. The First Aider got up and opened it. A police sergeant looked in.

'Ah, you're both here,' he said in relief. 'Call-out, Parry; there's a plane crashed on Y Garn. They heard it in Nebo flying very low and some people saw it go in. We're on the blower now at the station, trying to find out what's missing, but it's a plane all right; they heard the engines stop and the sound of the impact. There was a brilliant flash too.'

'Let's hope it's not a big one.' Gareth took his boots from under the table.

'Not likely to be any left alive,' the sergeant agreed. 'Your phone's not working, Mr Lloyd; been trying to get you for five minutes; thought you were out till I saw the 'Rover outside.'

'It didn't ring,' Gareth said.

'Shooting, Parry?' The sergeant was eyeing the shotgun.

'That's mine,' Gareth said quickly. 'Borrowed it from Colonel Grainger. What scheduled air routes are there over here? Irish, could it be?' He whisked a guard in front of the fire and, with a reflex action, snatched the hearth rug away.

'Probably something from Belfast,' the policeman said: 'Or Dublin. It was too slow for a jet though.'

'Have you called out the lads?' Gareth

asked, moving to the door.

'They're assembling at the Station.'

'It's a glorious night,' Parry said, holding the garage doors open for Gareth. He put his hand on the window and checked the other as he started to reverse. 'This is your show tonight, Gareth.'

'Oh no. You take charge while you're here.'

Parry grinned thinly. 'All right; but I'll leave the First Aid to you, you poor sod.'

CHAPTER SEVENTEEN

When they reached Nebo, which was a few miles from Minera, the village constable was waiting for them. Minera had come through on the telephone, he said, and a Dove was overdue on a run from Dublin to Manchester with eleven people aboard including the crew. The pilot had reported his position when over Liverpool Bay but since then there had been no further contact with Manchester.

The villagers said the aircraft had crashed about ten o'clock. A number of younger men had gone up from Nebo, the constable told them. Someone remarked *sotto voce* that now they'd be searching all night for the village lads.

There was no path. They set out on a direct route for the skyline. As they moved off, Parry told Gareth to go ahead with the First Aid rucksack. 'If you find we're holding you back,' he added. It was the first time he'd admitted that the other could move fast but it was a sensible decision for Gareth soon left the team behind.

There was a fairly steep ascent immediately above the village, then a levelling, with the steepest rise coming before the skyline.

The first gradient took its toll on Parry and he could feel the man behind him almost on his heels. He pushed himself, familiar with the agony of this initial burst of speed. The body was unwilling but driving it could do no harm; they'd soon settle to a steady rhythm, and if that was still too fast, he could recover when the ground levelled and he found his second wind for the last rise.

Tonight he could put no distance between himself and that second man: not even those few extra yards which would give him the encouragement to keep ahead. Bearing right on a diagonal line he glanced down and saw that he had no stragglers; he was holding them back. This had never happened before and he tried to concentrate on his breathing and the need to lift his legs faster. His chest hurt but it always hurt on quick spurts: racked by the compulsion to gulp great drafts of air—and the air was cold. He thanked God for the good night; they couldn't have had it better, only the body, his body, was at fault in its sluggishness.

At last he managed to get some more drive to his legs and on the next diagonal he saw that he'd gained a few yards on the others.

His lead increased and he felt a sweet elation. He had the edge on them. The line behind him started to straggle. He wondered how many men he could find in a remote Scottish glen to do this kind of thing—and the rest. Aircraft crashes were demoralising; the team killed themselves to get there in case there were survivors, but Minera had never been lucky in that respect, and no wonder—with the speed at which planes were flying when they struck.

They came to the top of the rise and the gradient ran out in a high corrie containing a lake. He didn't pause but kept going at a good pace. Despite this his lungs started to recover. Behind him the line closed up again but he guessed they'd left some stragglers toiling up the slope.

They were over the level ground too quickly, their shadows dancing before them with the moon at their backs. Parry saw the last slope ahead of him with rocks showing pale in the light. Again he went up in zigzags, drawing on the last reserves of energy. Gareth must be going well; they hadn't seen a sign of him.

Curiously, this rise didn't seem so bad as the first. His body responded splendidly; he could even take a pride in it: approving it in his mind for being so accommodating, despite his age, despite the whisky. He allowed the distance to contract between himself and the second man and, summoning his breath, said on a turn: 'We're doing well, should catch the village lads up any time.'

'Man,' the other gasped: 'You're going like a bomb; can't you slacken off a bit?'

'We're nearly there,' Parry said.

They came out on the top, but it was only the top of the slope. The moor rose gently ahead. He stopped and let the rest of the team collect, hearing their gasps and murmurs of protest but ignoring them. He counted heads and when they were all there, led the way across the moor. He realised now that he had made a mistake; he should have sent a radio operator with Gareth. He hadn't wanted to burden the other with a set when he was carrying the First Aid rucksack. Now they had no way of telling where the First Aider might be. If they went to the knoll ahead would they be able to see enough ground in the moonlight to spot the crash?

There was very rough ground between them and the knoll. They struggled up to their knees in peat hags, the mud sucking at their boots, and occasionally, when one foot was on a tussock and the other in a hole, someone fell. He heard them thrashing behind him and prayed that the little rise would give him a view.

He was first on the top and looking round

he saw, some distance away, a weak light that was too low for a star. As the next man joined him, Parry sent him back to tell the lads to be quiet, then he shouted. The reply came loudly: 'Over here!' and the light described an arc as it was waved.

There was more bog, and between the bogs there was deep heather above rocks and holes in which a man could break a leg. They could see now that the ground rose behind the man with the light and it occurred to Parry that they weren't at the site of the crash; that they'd merely found the villagers who were lost themselves. Were they to be condemned to a night of sweep-searching?

As they approached, the light disappeared and he had a momentary qualm before he realised that the man who'd been directing them had turned and was moving away. They started to overhaul him and came over a hump to see, in the saucer beyond, the aircraft like a monstrous beetle with its wings torn off and the body ripped in half.

It seemed oddly silent because they'd expected a loud bustle of activity but then their ears picked up the lesser sounds—of splashing. Men were wading round the wreck and one was climbing gingerly into the torn fuselage.

Parry was about to tell the team to find Gareth when he saw that they were already hurrying past him. Even as he wondered why he wasn't hurrying too, his legs buckled under him and he collapsed to the ground. 'Like being drunk,' he said aloud. No one seemed to have noticed; they were all ahead of him now.

He knew that he should get up and join the others but he was afraid that if he collapsed again he might fall in the water face down and drown. This was a problem that had to be worked out but his brain seemed lazy. The sense of urgency had gone.

He observed the scene before him with detachment. There seemed to be little urgency about that either. Men were wading in the water, apparently feeling with their feet. The water was very shallow; it wasn't a lake. Presumably they were feeling for bodies. It was unlikely that there were any survivors because they would have been moved to dry ground. He looked along the margin on either side of him and could discern no stooping figures tending victims. It was better that they should have died quickly.

On his left was a shallow pool, a rock showing on its edge below the overhanging bank. There were reeds in the pool and they moved slightly in the breeze. He was sweating profusely; he could have done with a touch of that breeze. So why didn't he feel it, why should it be so localised?

He looked at the pool with sharper eyes. The reeds had stopped moving. Had they moved? There was movement now—again. The rock? *Rock?*

He tried to get up but his legs wouldn't bear his weight. He slid his arms out of the rucksack straps and eased over on his chest, then he started to crawl through the heather, dragging his legs.

It was a long journey. He came to the top of the bank and below him a piece had given way and there was a peaty depression down to the water. What had been a rock, he saw now, was a body, half-submerged on the remains of the bank. It was lying face down seemingly supported on one arm. The other arm moved weakly in the water—but there was no current.

Parry drew himself to the lip of the depression and, grasping the heather, worked his legs round. For a moment he lay there and then he forced himself to kick at the slimy bank. He hadn't enough strength to do that so, letting the heather go but clutching at the slime with his hands and using his fingers as a brake, he slid down the channel.

There were only a few feet to go. His boots touched the bottom and he toppled sideways into the water. Up on hands and knees again he reached out and touched the other's hand. The head lifted wearily.

'Help me!' It was a girl's voice.

Parry stood up and lifted her. She was astonishingly light, only a child surely because she was so short: more like a dwarf.

He couldn't carry her up the bank so he waded along underneath it to where the shore was level and fringed with turf. He put her down carefully and she thanked him. His legs betrayed him again and he sank beside her.

'Where's the pain?' he asked.

'No pain.' It was a whisper.

'That's fine.' If she'd been flung out of the aircraft it would probably be the back. If she'd crawled out of the fuselage she must have some injuries after the shock of the impact, even if she'd managed to crawl this far.

Something was happening over by the wreck. There was an outburst of orders and he noticed that more men had arrived on the scene. He saw two carrying a stretcher, black against the light. He shouted to them and was surprised to hear the weakness in his voice. No one paid any attention. The stretcher was being taken across to the fuselage. Something plucked his sleeve. He turned and was startled to see how mature her face seemed for a child.

'How did you get out?' she asked.

'I'm a rescuer.' It recalled him to the business in hand. The back. If she couldn't move her legs . . .

He eased away from her slightly and dragged himself forward again. 'Can you wriggle your toes?'

If she answered, he didn't hear her. He was staring at the grass where there shouldn't be grass. As he fumbled for the switch of his headlight he was praying that it was an illusion, that she'd been born like this . . . a thalidomide baby . . . ?

The light came on and he saw the wounds. She was neither dwarf nor child but a girl who had lost both legs.

'What's the light?' she asked. 'Is it the moon?'

'My torch.' He eased himself back beside her and now his wrists gave way. As he slumped he managed to turn so that he was lying on his back.

'Can you see the moon now?' he whispered.

'Yes. You've hurt yourself, haven't you?'

He didn't answer.

Above him he could see the bright glow of light across the sky but the moon itself was just at the edge of his vision. He felt no pain and no discomfort. Something touched his hand and closed on it. He couldn't turn his head, could acknowledge the gesture in no way, but he appreciated it.

He could hear the sound of activity in the distance, heard them shouting his name. Beside him she started to breathe loudly and shakily as if there were an obstruction in her throat. Her hand tightened on his, the breathing stopped and then the fingers slackened a little.

Voices approached and the soft thud of feet in the heather.

'There's a light!'

'Where?'

'On the ground. He's got to be—Heh, this is

two more . . .'

'It's him, you fool. Parry, wake up, Parry!'

'God, what the hell's wrong with him? Is he drunk? Where's Gareth?'

'Gareth!'

'This is a girl. She must have been thrown clear. She's dead. Oh Christ, she's got no—'

'But what happened to Parry? His eyes are open. He must have left his light on when he felt himself going . . .'

'Come out of it, Evans; let me get to him.'

'Is he dead, Gareth?'

'Where's it hurt, Owen? Can't move anything?'

Capable hands explored his body. 'Feel that? Close your eyes for yes. You can do that? Good. Feel this? Pulled one out of the water, did you? You're a hard man, Parry.'

Gareth stood up and turned, giving orders in a low voice. Others were collecting slowly about them. A bear-like figure loomed beside the First Aider. That could only be Simon. The two had their heads together and Simon's face was turned towards him.

'No, you tell him; better he should know.'

Gareth squatted. 'It's probably a slight stroke, Owen, but you're going to be all right. I've sent the only survivor down already but there's another stretcher on the way; it shouldn't be long.'

They lifted him and put their anoraks between him and the ground, then covered him with sweaters. Gareth bent over him. 'Is there anything I can do for you?' Parry kept his eyes open. The other looked towards the moor and then at Simon who must have moved the girl's body because he was kneeling on the other side. Parry saw that they were clamping down on anxiety in order not to alarm himself and the team. He concentrated on the muscles round his mouth so that he could reassure them with some movement of the lips that might resemble a smile. He didn't think he could put pleasure in his eyes; those would either be frightened or not frightened and if the latter, the others would merely think he wasn't fully aware of the situation.

Trying to recover movement was extremely difficult but he came to realise that if he couldn't reassure them of his comfort, no harm would be done; Simon, Gareth—and indeed the team—had the resources to cope with compassion.

The stretcher arrived and they put him in the casualty bag. As they moved him the night scenes were imprinted on his brain. There was the marsh like mercury with the broken aircraft in the centre; there was a rock wall of indeterminate size and irrelevant angle but probably vertical with the light slicing it cleanly, leaving half in shadow below the mountain humped against the sky.

They strapped him on the stretcher, working with the deftness which he had

272

watched for years and never appreciated.

They lifted him and started down: over the moor, avoiding the peat hags, to the lip of the gradient that overlooked the valley where the village lay in another world. Somewhere between village and mountain was a line: at a thousand feet, two thousand, or only in the mind, below which the odds were loaded against you, but once above the line wherever it might be, once the quiet places were reached, the odds were loaded the other way because the demons could not associate with beauty.

Ugliness was in the mind, and other dark things, and you'd think a stroke at forty would be the ultimate blow. It was, of course; now he'd lost everything except that trickle of life which reached no farther than his eyelids— and he was glad of it. Everything had gone, for what it was worth, and the empty vessel could start to fill again.

All the way down to the road he lay and watched the sky, observed the moon bob in and out of the moving bodies, listened to their breathing, their foot-falls on earth crackling with frost, and he realised how much he adored his world. Lying stricken and serene among his men he was deeply grateful, unafraid, and even a little amused. The demons were neither gone nor vanquished but from this point on he knew that they could only be as dreadful as he made them.